LES SABLES MOUVANTS

SHIFTINC SANDS

Hubert Aquin
5159 Notre-Dame-de-Grâce
Montréal 260

LES SABLES MOUVANTS

SHIFTING SANDS

HUBERT AQUIN

Translation with Notes & a Critical Essay
by Joseph Jones

RONSDALE PRESS

RONSDALE PRESS
3350 West 21st Avenue, Vancouver, B.C., Canada v6s 1G7
www.ronsdalepress.com

Typesetting: Julie Cochrane, in Granjon 11.5 on 18pt
Cover Art & Design: David Drummond
Paper: Ancient Forest Friendly "Silva" (FSC) — 100% post-consumer waste, totally chlorine-free and acid-free

Ronsdale Press wishes to thank the following for their support of its publishing program: the Canada Council for the Arts, the Government of Canada through the Book Publishing Industry Development Program (BPIDP), the British Columbia Arts Council, and the Province of British Columbia through the British Columbia Book Publishing Tax Credit program.

Library and Archives Canada Cataloguing in Publication

Aquin, Hubert, 1929–1977
[Sables mouvants. English & French]
    Les sables mouvants: nouvelle = Shifting sands: novella / Hubert Aquin; translated by Joseph Jones.

Original French text and English translation.
Includes bibliographical references.
ISBN 978-1-55380-078-1

    1. Jones, Joseph, 1947–   II. Title.   III. Title: Shifting sands.
    IV. Sables mouvants. English & French

PS8501.Q85S23 2009   C843'.54   C2009-905460-4E

Catalogage avant publication de Bibliothèque et Archives Canada

Aquin, Hubert, 1929–1977
[Sables mouvants. Anglais & français]
    Les sables mouvants: nouvelle = Shifting sands: novella / Hubert Aquin; translated by Joseph Jones.

Texte original français et traduction anglaise.
Comprend des références bibliographiques.
ISBN 978-1-55380-078-1

    1. Jones, Joseph, 1947–   II. Titre.   III. Titre: Shifting sands.
    IV. Sables mouvants. Anglais & français

PS8501.Q85S23 2009   C843'.54   C2009-905460-4F

Printed in Canada by Marquis Printing, Québec

CONTENTS

∽

Appréciation de Marie-Claire Blais ▪ 6

Appreciation by Marie-Claire Blais ▪ 7

First Leaf of the Typescript / Première feuille du tapuscrit ▪ 8

Les sables mouvants / Shifting Sands ▪ 9

Note on the Title ▪ 71

The Maleficent Vision and *Shifting Sands*: A Critical Essay ▪ 75

Notes on the Edition and Translation ▪ 97

Annotations ▪ 99

Notes sur le texte / Notes on the Text ▪ 101

Hubert Aquin (1929–1977) ▪ 106

APPRÉCIATION
DE MARIE-CLAIRE BLAIS

ON RETROUVE DANS cette nouvelle toute l'âme sensible du grand écrivain, la poignante sincérité d'un être souvent écorché à vif mais qui refuse toute consolation, toute protection nuisant à sa fierté de vivre et de mourir. Ici, c'est l'amour d'une femme qui élève, tourmente, glorifie ou abat celui qui l'attend, l'espère, la crée et la recrée dans la solitude, avec des images d'une beauté aussi mouvante que sensuelle.

Mais plus que le récit d'un amour en fuite, ce qui nous touche tant, dans cette nouvelle digne de la *Métamorphose* de Kafka et s'en rapprochant par le ton, l'élégance et le désespoir, c'est ce cri qui monte de la captivité intérieure de son auteur. Voici l'auteur d'une métamorphose amoureuse, enfermé entre les murs d'une chambre d'hôtel étrangère, en ce lieu étranger où il lutte contre lui-même, dans les souterrains de son être, pétrissant sa conscience de ces mots, vivre ou aimer, aimer ou mourir, mais se sentant si écrasé, si démuni qu'il croit entendre sonner en lui, ainsi que chez les personnages de Kafka, le glas de la sentence de vivre, comme celui de la délivrance par la mort.

Mais n'oublions pas, par ailleurs, qu'il y avait parfois, par instants rares, un humour, une joie chez Hubert Aquin, ou bien plutôt une légèreté mozartienne qui n'étaient qu'à lui.

APPRECIATION
BY MARIE-CLAIRE BLAIS

IN THIS NOVELLA the reader encounters the entire sensitive soul of this great writer, the heart-rending sincerity of a being often flayed alive yet one who refuses all consolation, all protection that might hurt his pride in living and dying. Here, it is the love of a woman that lifts up, torments, glorifies or casts down the one who waits for her, hopes for her, creates and recreates her in solitude, with images of a beauty just as fluid as sensual.

But more than the story of a love in flight, what touches us so much, in this novella worthy of Kafka's *Metamorphosis* and approaching it in tone, elegance and despair, is this cry that arises from the inner captivity of its author. Behold the author of an amorous metamorphosis, shut in by the walls of a foreign hotel room, in this foreign place where he struggles against himself, in the hidden depths of his being, moulding his consciousness with these words, live or love, love or die, but feeling so crushed, so dispossessed that he thinks he hears toll in himself, as do Kafka's characters, the bell of the sentence to live, like that of deliverance through death.

But let us not forget, in other respects, that there was sometimes, in unusual moments, a humour, a joy in Hubert Aquin, or indeed rather a Mozartian lightness that was his alone.

44P-660.02/2   *1955*

Les Sables mouvants

1...

Je suis coincé entre les quatre murs du souvenir, dans une chambre
humide et basse. Je n'ose pas regarder par cette fenêtre. Ça me donne
l'impression que je suis dans une cave. Tout se passe au-dessus de
moi. Je vois des jambes courir devant la fenêtre. Décidément, elle
est très haute. Si je devais m'enfuir, il serait tellement facile de
m'écraser les mains, deme broyer les doigts. Et je retomberais dans
mon trou. Je suis pris dans une sorte de fosse d'où j'aperçois encore
les jambes des fossoyeurs et des amis. Le couvercle va peut-être se
refermer, je resterai seul avec mon humidité, seul dans cette chambre
d'hôtel qui ressemble à un salon mortuaire, seul à attendre la vermine.
L'endroit est propice à cela, je l'ai tout de suite compris. Déjà je
me sens pénétré, il y a des choses qui travaillent sur mon corps. On
entre en moi lentement.

Je regrette maintenant d'avoir choisi Naples. Il y a tellement d'autres
villes où nous aurions pu nous rencontrer. Florence, Rome, Milan même.
Naples, évidemment, c'est un nom magique. Je voyais tout de suite les
sérénades, les promenades au port le soir, le soleil. Elle était enchantée,
elle aussi. Naples, c'était la grande aventure. Tant pis. Je n'aurais
pas le temps de lui écrire que je préfère l'attendre à Rome. Elle est
déjà partie. Non pas encore, presque. Demain matin, à 9 heures , elle
prend le train à la gare de Lyon. 24 heures pour Rome, puis , en prenant
le direttissimo, elle sera ici à 1.40. Je lui ai tout expliqué.

Décidément, c'est malsain ici. Ma chemise s'alourdit sur moi. Quand je
m'étends sur le lit, c'est pire, je deviens comme écœuré: je n'ai plus
le goût de rien faire. Mes forces s'effritent. Même lire m'ennuie. J'ai

First leaf of the typescript / Première feuille du tapuscrit

Les sables mouvants

Shifting Sands

JE SUIS COINCÉ ENTRE les quatre murs du souvenir, dans une chambre humide et basse. Je n'ose pas regarder par cette fenêtre. Ça me donne l'impression que je suis dans une cave. Tout se passe au-dessus de moi. Je vois des jambes courir devant la fenêtre. Décidément, elle est très haute. Si je devais m'enfuir, il serait tellement facile de m'écraser les mains, de me broyer les doigts. Et je retomberais dans mon trou. Je suis pris dans une sorte de fosse d'où j'aperçois encore les jambes des fossoyeurs et des amis. Le couvercle va peut-être se refermer, je resterai seul avec mon humidité, seul dans cette chambre d'hôtel qui ressemble à un salon mortuaire, seul à attendre la vermine. L'endroit est propice à cela, je l'ai tout de suite compris. Déjà je me sens pénétré, il y a des choses qui travaillent sur mon corps. On entre en moi lentement.

I'M CAUGHT BETWEEN THE four walls of memory, in a damp low room. I don't dare look through this window. It gives me the feeling of being in a cellar. Everything happens above me. I see legs hurry past the window. Really, it's very high. If I had to escape, it would be so easy to get my hands trampled, my fingers crushed. And I'd fall back into my hole. I'm trapped in a kind of grave where I still see the legs of gravediggers and friends. Maybe the lid will close again, I'll be left alone with my dampness, alone in this hotel room that resembles a funeral parlor, alone to wait for the bugs. The place is suited for that; I understood that right away. Already I feel penetrated. There are things that are working on my body. They enter me slowly.

Je regrette maintenant d'avoir choisi Naples. Il y a tellement d'autres villes où nous aurions pu nous rencontrer. Florence, Rome, Milan même. Naples, évidemment, c'est un nom magique. Je voyais tout de suite les sérénades, les promenades au port le soir, le soleil. Elle était enchantée, elle aussi. Naples, c'était la grande aventure. Tant pis. Je n'aurais pas le temps de lui écrire que je préfère l'attendre à Rome. Elle est déjà partie. Non pas encore, presque. Demain matin, à 9 heures, elle prend le train à la gare de Lyon. 24 heures pour Rome, puis, en prenant le direttissimo, elle sera ici à 1.40. Je lui ai tout expliqué.

Décidément, c'est malsain ici. Ma chemise s'alourdit sur moi. Quand je m'étends sur le lit, c'est pire, je deviens comme écoeuré : je n'ai le goût de rien faire. Mes forces s'effritent. Même lire m'ennuie. J'ai d'ailleurs presque terminé le Stendhal. Dieu sait si cela peut être ennuyant des impressions de voyage en Italie. On voit bien qu'il n'attendait pas, lui. Il regardait tout simplement ; il rentrait chez lui le soir et racontait ce qu'il avait vu. Il n'était pas impatient ou inquiet. Il n'attendait personne à Naples, sinon . . . Deux jours. Deux jours, mais après un mois. Et surtout dans cette chambre. Il faudra changer d'ailleurs, car Hélène ne coucherait pas ici. Nous quitterons Naples au plus vite à son arrivée ; moi j'en aurai assez. Nous trouverons une petite auberge, près de Sorrento. Mais pas cette chambre, pas ces murs. Ces murs bruns laids. Il y a même des dessins de fleurs. Elles ressemblent plutôt à des araignées. Sur les quatre murs et de bas en haut, elles étendent leurs grandes pattes. Au plafond, ce sont les vraies araignées. Ma foi, il y a des fils partout, entre les tuyaux et le mur, dans l'encadrure de cette porte barrée. Cette fausse porte d'ailleurs déplairait à Hélène. C'est comme si

Now I regret having chosen Naples. There are so many other cities where we could have met. Florence, Rome, even Milan. Naples, obviously that's a magic name. Right away I envisioned serenades, strolls at the port in the evening, the sun. She was enchanted too. Naples, that was the great adventure. Too bad. I wouldn't have time to write her that I'd prefer to wait for her in Rome. She's already left. No, not yet, almost. Tomorrow morning, at nine o'clock, she catches the train at the Lyon station. Twenty-four hours to Rome; then, taking the direttissimo, she'll be here at 1:40. I explained all that to her.

Really, it is unhealthy here. My shirt weighs on me. When I stretch out on the bed, it's worse, I feel sick: I don't want to do anything. My strength crumbles. Even reading bores me. Besides, I have almost finished the Stendhal. God knows it can get boring, with those impressions of travel in Italy. You can see that he wasn't waiting, not him. He just looked; he went home in the evening and recounted what he had seen. He wasn't impatient or anxious. But then, he wasn't waiting for anyone in Naples . . . Two days. Two days, but after a month. And especially in this room. We'll have to change anyway, because Hélène wouldn't spend the night here. We'll leave Naples as fast as we can when she arrives; I'll certainly have had enough. We'll find a little inn, near Sorrento. But not this room, not these walls. These ugly brown walls. There are even flower patterns. They look more like spiders. On the four walls and from bottom to top, they spread their big legs. On the ceiling, those are actual spiders. My goodness, there are cobwebs everywhere, between the pipes and the wall, in the frame of this locked door. This fake door would be something else to bother Hélène. It's as if someone

quelqu'un pouvait entrer d'un moment à l'autre et nous surprendre. C'est une menace perpétuelle, et si je continuais de la regarder, je sens que je ne pourrais fermer l'oeil de la nuit. Pourtant, elle doit être barrée. Mais une porte, on ne peut oublier que cela reste une porte: une porte blanche, mal peinturée, avec un trou de serrure. Regardons par le trou. On l'a bouché probablement, c'est noir. Je me souviens la première fois qu'Hélène est venue à ma chambre. C'est ce qui lui avait déplu: la porte, juste en face du lit. Je lui ai répété que jamais elle ne s'ouvrait, que jamais à ma connaissance elle n'avait été ouverte, que jamais de toute éternité quelqu'un ne passerait ce seuil. Elle ne l'aimait pas. Elle l'a regardée tout le temps qu'elle est restée dans la chambre. Elle ne pouvait pas s'y habituer. Elle est revenue par la suite. Deux fois. Non, trois fois. C'etait pour m'aider à faire mes valises. On ne pensait plus à la porte alors. Hélène y pensait peut-être. On n'en parlait plus en tout cas. D'ailleurs ensemble nous n'avons jamais beaucoup parlé, il faut bien le dire. Même la première fois que je l'ai vue.

On a commencé en silence. Je n'ai jamais bien compris son comportement ce soir-là. A quel moment, ai-je senti que quelque chose se passait, que nos relations se transformaient. Même pas. J'ai à peine deviné la complicité de son regard. On se regardait si peu de face. Une sorte de certitude m'assurait qu'Hélène n'était plus la même. A quoi attribuer ce revirement de sa part. Car moi je lui avais fait savoir trop souvent qu'elle me plaisait. Et avec quelle maladresse. Je n'osais plus escompter un succès que j'avais désiré avec trop de rage. J'avais toujours le dessous avec elle. C'est moi qui me fourvoyais en paroles, en explications, en commentaires. Elle ne disait jamais un mot. Elle régnait sur une montagne que je gravissais péniblement pour la

could come in at any moment and surprise us. It's a constant threat, and if I were to keep on looking at it, I feel as though I wouldn't be able to close my eyes at night. Nevertheless, it must be locked. But a door, you can't forget that it is still a door: a white door, poorly painted, with a keyhole. Let's look through the hole. They've probably stopped it up, it's black. I remember the first time Hélène came to my room. That's what bothered her: the door, just opposite the bed. I told her over and over that it would never open, that never to my knowledge had it been opened, that never in all eternity would anyone cross that sill. She didn't like it. She looked at it the whole time she was staying in the room. She couldn't get used to it. She came back later on. Twice. No, three times. That was to help me pack my bags. No more thought was given to the door then. Hélène thought of it, maybe. Anyway, we didn't talk about it any more. Besides, we never talked much when we were together. That's a fact. Even the first time that I saw her.

We began in silence. I've never really understood her behaviour that evening. At what moment did I sense that something was happening, that our relationship was changing. Not even that. I scarcely picked up on the complicity of her look. So little did we look directly at each other. A kind of certainty assured me that Hélène was no longer the same. What might be the cause of this sudden change of direction on her part. For my part I had too often let her know that I found her attractive. And with what awkwardness. I no longer dared to count on a success that I had desired with too much frenzy. I always came off the worse with her. I was the one who went astray with speeches, explanations, comments. She never said a word. She held sway over a mountain that I was painfully climbing to catch up

rejoindre, puis finalement je trébuchais et je dévalais toute la pente. Devant les autres, je devenais plus maladroit. Je détruisais tous mes effets avant même de m'en servir . . .

Qu'y avait-il de changé ce soir-là? J'étais le même, peut-être désinvolte, car j'en étais venu à me moquer d'une ambition à jamais vaine. A un certain moment dans la soirée, après le repas, quelque chose est arrivé, un changement de densité. Elle m'écoutait parler et me donnait toujours raison. Cela m'autorisa à produire mes idées encore plus cavalièrement: elle confirmait toujours, elle approuvait, elle disait toujours: "C'est vrai" . . . C'était mon soir. Les évènements tournaient en ma faveur. Il était près de minuit, et j'étais décidé à ne pas partir de chez elle. J'avais hâte que l'heure du dernier métro fût passée pour m'aider de ce prétexte. Vers minuit et demi, je remarquai d'évidents signes de nervosité chez elle. Moi, j'étais à vide de conversation, et nous écoutions en silence marquer les secondes à l'horloge. Nous étions très nerveux tous les deux. Mon coeur faisait tous le temps dans ma poitrine. Je n'avais rien dit encore à Hélène pour la séduire. L'heure passait, j'étais sauf, seul avec Hélène dans une chambre, sur un même canapé. Tout paraissait évident quoique, pour moi, inespéré.

Je pris quelques minutes pour reprendre mon aplomb. J'appliquai toute mon énergie à dissimuler mon ravissement. Je parlai un peu, trop, sûrement. Il se passa un bon 15 minutes de malaise. Puis, risquant le tout pour le tout, sans transition aucune, sans le préambule habituel de la douceur et de la tendresse, je me levai pour fermer la lumière. Elle ne disait toujours pas un mot. Moi non plus. J'avais pourtant quelques boutades qui me brûlaient la langue. Cette scène était décidément comique. Je me frappai contre le lit en revenant, je pris ma place, je relevai sur nous une couverture que j'avais remarquée d'abord,

with her, then finally I tripped and tumbled all the way down the slope. In front of others, I became more clumsy. I destroyed all my good impressions even before taking advantage of them . . .

What was there that had changed that evening? I was the same, perhaps off-hand, because I had gotten to the point of making fun of an ambition that was forever futile. At a certain moment in the evening, after the meal, something happened, a change in atmosphere. She listened to me talk and always agreed with me. That permitted me to put forth my ideas still more flippantly: she always confirmed, she approved, she always said: "That's right" . . . It was my evening. Events were turning in my favour. It was almost midnight, and I had decided not to leave her place. I was eager to run out of time for the last metro, to make use of this pretext. Toward 12:30, I noticed obvious signs of nervousness on her part. Me, I had run out of conversation, and we listened in silence to the clock marking the seconds. We were both very nervous. My heart was pounding in my chest. I still had said nothing to Hélène to seduce her. The time was passing, I was safe, alone with Hélène in a room, on the same couch. Everything seemed obvious, although, for me, unhoped for.

I took a few minutes to regain my composure. I put all my energy into concealing my delight. I talked a little, too much for sure. A good fifteen minutes of discomfort went by. Then, risking everything, without any transition, without the usual preamble of sweetness and affection, I got up to turn off the light. She still didn't say a word. Neither did I. Still, I had several facetious remarks at the tip of my tongue. This scene was definitely comical. I bumped against the bed coming back, I took my place, I pulled a coverlet over us

et tentai de reconnaître les lieux de son corps pour m'y conformer. Je rencontrai d'abord son visage dont le contact me fut infiniment doux, cette peau lisse et brûlante que j'avais à peine effleurée quelques fois en dansant et qui tout d'un coup m'était offerte. Je reconnus le coin de la bouche et les lèvres. Je posai, à tout hasard et comme par principe, quelques baisers sur ce visage avec lequel je n'étais pas encore familier. Je passai tant bien que mal une jambe par-dessus les siennes. Je mettais du temps à prendre ma position. Tout cela se faisait en silence, nous ne prononcions pas un traître mot. Je l'embrassai sur les lèvres. J'avais un peu de difficulté à rendre ces baisers faciles: je tournais et retournais ma tête pour trouver l'harmonie parfaite. Je commençais par les commissures, je me rapprochais du centre, je relevais ses lèvres et je passais ma langue. Je sentis enfin l'accord se produire. Ses lèvres remuaient avec les miennes, je sentis sa salive pénétrer dans ma bouche et nos langues s'effleurer avec douceur, se tenir un langage nouveau et capiteux. Puis je me retirais; nos lèvres étaient encore mouillées de salive, et nous reprenions ces étreintes qui étaient nos premiers gestes.

Le moment n'était pas encore venu de me laisser aller à mon ravissement et d'avouer un plaisir qui m'aurait, encore une fois, fait perdre le dessus. C'est son ravissement que je voulais le premier. Je l'embrassai dans le cou. La devinant consentante, je pris une initiative qui aurait dû être une douce découverte, mais qui était alors une gageure. Je dégrafai les deux épaisseurs qui la couvraient. Elle ne dit pas un mot, moi non plus par principe. Elle se laissait faire, et moi j'allais d'autant plus lentement que la chose me semblait ridicule. Je me rendis jusqu'au bout de la rangée de boutons, j'écartai les vêtements et j'embrassai ses seins. Quelle merveilleuse sensation de toucher cette poitrine palpitante et ouverte à mes lèvres. Je la couvrais de mes lèvres. J'aurais voulu que son sang affluât

that I had noticed at the outset, and tried to recognize the places of her body to match myself to. First I encountered her face, whose touch was for me infinitely soft, this smooth and burning skin that I had barely brushed against several times while dancing and which all of a sudden was offered to me. I recognized the corner of her mouth and her lips. Completely at random and as a matter of principle, I placed some kisses on this face that I wasn't yet well acquainted with. Somehow I managed to throw a leg over hers. I spent some time finding my position. All this was done in silence, we didn't breathe a word. I kissed her on the lips. I had a little difficulty in making those kisses artful: I turned and turned my head to find perfect harmony. I started at the corners of her mouth, I moved toward the center, I opened her lips and put in my tongue. Finally I sensed her consent. Her lips moved with mine, I felt her saliva enter my mouth and our tongues brush gently, a new and sensuous language taking place. Then I withdrew; our lips were still moist with saliva, and we resumed those embraces that were our first moves.

The moment hadn't yet come to let myself go in my ecstasy and to admit to a pleasure that would have, once again, made me lose the upper hand. It was her ecstasy that I wanted first. I kissed her on the neck. Feeling her willing, I made a move that should have been a welcome discovery but was then a long shot. I unfastened the two layers that covered her. She didn't say a word, me neither as a matter of principle. She kept still, and me, I went even slower as it all struck me as ridiculous. I proceeded to the end of the row of buttons, opened her clothes and kissed her breasts. What a marvellous sensation to touch them, alive and open to my lips. I put my lips everywhere. I felt as if her blood should flow in me and overrun me.

en moi et m'inondât. Je l'embrassais à lui rompre la peau. J'aspirais ses seins brûlants: c'était mon pain et mon vin, ma nourriture la plus indispensable . . .

Je commence à ressentir des douleurs dans le dos. Il faut bien venir à Naples au mois de mai pour souffrir de l'humidité. Je ne devrais pas refaire sans cesse mon passé. J'ai peur de ne pouvoir rattraper tout ce que j'ai fait. Une bonne fois, il m'arrivera de m'arrêter en chemin, de bloquer quelque part. Il me tarde de finir cette nuit pour m'assurer qu'elle est bien passée . . . J'ai peur qu'elle ne soit pas encore finie et que je reste accroché pour toujours à un souvenir défectueux. Où en étais-je. J'ai de la difficulté à reprendre. Il y a pourtant un dénouement, une fin. Je me souviens du lendemain matin quand je pris le métro . . . Je riais. Je riais, je ne pouvais pas m'arrêter. Oui, je m'arrêtais. Et tout à coup, insolemment, j'éclatais à nouveau chaque fois que je revoyais ma nuit avec Hélène. En la quittant, juste avant, je m'étais appliqué à être le plus froid possible, à éteindre toute démonstration. C'est toujours ce qui m'a désarçonné avec Hélène: cette lourdeur de l'effusion, cette gêne (est-elle physique ou autre) à exprimer les sentiments les plus convenus. Il n'y a que ses yeux qui parlent sans affectation, mais les yeux c'est la chose au monde à laquelle on peut le moins se fier . . . Elle n'a pas ces gestes relâchés et insouciants qui précèdent la pensée dans les moments de passion. Elle n'étreint jamais irrésistiblement. Cette nuit-là je devais me fier à sa respiration pour mesurer son acquiescement. J'écoutais le rythme coupé de son souffle et je savais si mon geste portait juste, et si ma main pressait assez fort . . . Dieu que je riais. Les gens me regardaient dans le métro. J'avais le goût de taper tout le monde sur l'épaule. J'étais content. La fierté avait eu son compte. Enfin, s'agissait-il de fierté. Cela rendait toute émotion impossible.

I kissed her enough to break her skin. I inhaled her burning breasts: this was my bread and my wine, my most indispensable food . . .

I'm starting to feel pain in my back. Nothing like coming to Naples in the month of May to suffer from the humidity. I shouldn't go over my past incessantly. I'm afraid of not being able to recapture everything I have done. Someday I'll wind up stopped on the road, stuck somewhere. I'm anxious to finish this night to assure myself that it is really over . . . I'm afraid that it isn't finished yet and that I'll stay hung up forever on a faulty memory. Where was I? It's hard to get started again. There is however a conclusion, an end. I remember the next morning when I took the metro . . . I was laughing. I was laughing, I couldn't stop myself. Yes, I did stop. And all of a sudden, insolently, I burst out again each time I went over my night with Hélène. Just before leaving her I worked at being as cold as possible, at extinguishing every display of emotion. That is what always threw me with Hélène: that awkwardness in chatting, that discomfort (physical or otherwise) in expressing the most conventional feelings. Only her eyes speak without affectation, but the eyes are the least trustworthy thing in the world . . . She doesn't have those relaxed and carefree movements that come before thought in moments of passion. She never embraces irresistibly. That night I had to rely on her breathing to measure her acquiescence. I listened to its broken rhythm and I knew whether my move was appropriate, and whether my hand was pressing hard enough . . . God, how I laughed. People looked at me in the metro. I felt like tapping everyone on the shoulder. I was happy. Pride had had its reckoning. In the end, it was a matter of pride. That rendered all emotion impossible.

Inutile de sortir. Il pleut trop. Je reviendrais encore plus humide. Et je n'ai pas d'habit de rechange. Restons dans ces murs pour attendre la nuit. Etendons-nous peut-être. Sur le dos. Sur le dos, cela nous oblige à regarder les murs et le plafond. Je n'avais pas remarqué ces guirlandes de plâtre au plafond. De vrais nids d'araignées, quoi. Par un temps pareil, les araignées doivent s'en donner à coeur joie. C'est un jour d'araignées. Elles sortent de leur cachette et se pendent à leurs grands fils. Elles descendent le long des murs, lentement, puis je ne les distingue plus. Elles se dissimulent dans les fleurs brunes. Il y en a partout mais je ne les vois plus: cachées dans les fleurs, elles m'observent. La couleur n'est pas tellement différente, on confondrait aisément. Mais moi je guette. Je les vois remuer. Elles s'agitent sur les fleurs, et tout le mur ressemble à une forêt. Je vois des milliers de grandes pattes autour de moi et des fleurs qui bougent. Ce doit être le printemps sur les murs: il y a des germes partout; les fleurs s'allongent à vue d'oeil et viennent balancer au-dessus de ma tête. Je dors dans un champ d'araignées et je ne puis empêcher cette végétation affreuse autour de moi. Mes cheveux se prennent dans les tiges, je ne peux plus les démêler. Il y a des fils partout. Je sens des frôlements dans le cou. Ma peau va bientôt germer elle aussi et je deviendrai nid d'araignées . . .

Les fleurs ont changé ce matin. On dirait qu'elles sont bleues et plus grandes. Il fait soleil aujourd'hui. Il n'est que sept heures. Ce sera long. Et je ne m'endors même pas. Je passais mes mains sous son corps et je m'approchais d'elle. Qu'il fait bon de se retrouver ainsi le

No use going out. It's raining too much. I'd come back even wet-
ter. And I don't have a change of clothes. Let's stay within these walls
to await the night. Let's stretch out, perhaps. On our back. On our
back, that forces us to look at the walls and the ceiling. I hadn't
noticed these wreaths of plaster on the ceiling. Real nests of spiders,
I'd say. In this kind of weather, the spiders must be having a blast.
It's a day for spiders. They come out of their hiding place and dan-
gle on their long threads. They descend along the walls, slowly, then
I can no longer make them out. They conceal themselves in the
brown flowers. There are some everywhere but I no longer see them:
hidden in the flowers, they look at me. The colour isn't so different,
you would easily confuse them. But me, I keep an eye out. I see them
shifting around. They skitter on the flowers, and the entire wall looks
like a forest. I see thousands of big legs around me and flowers that
move. It must be springtime on the walls: there are seeds everywhere;
the flowers grow before my eyes and come to sway above my head.
I sleep in a field of spiders and I can't keep away this frightful vegetation around me. My hair gets caught in the stems, I can no longer
untangle it. There are strands everywhere. I feel things brushing
against my neck. Soon my skin is going to sprout as well and I will
become a nest of spiders . . .

The flowers have changed this morning. It looks like they are blue
and bigger. It's sunny today. It's only seven o'clock. It'll be a long day.
And I'm not even sleepy. I slipped my hands under her body and
came closer to her. How good it is to find each other like that in

matin. On s'était éloigné pendant la nuit sans le vouloir, et puis quand le jour est entré par la fenêtre, je me retournais vers elle et je la réveillais. Elle n'ouvrait même pas les yeux. Elle se plaignait un peu parce que je la déplaçais. Ses seins étaient encore plus chauds le matin, et son dos surtout. Je m'appuyais à ce balcon étrange qu'elle a aux flancs et où je restais pendu des heures de temps comme un désespéré. J'embrassais son ventre. Je me cramponnais à cette montagne comme si le vertige m'eût pris et que je craignisse de tomber dans le vide. J'enfonçais mes mains dans ce roc brûlé par le soleil et je mouillais son ventre de ma salive. Parfois j'effleurais cette noire forêt, cette végétation fière, cette crinière plus farouche que les cheveux. Je me souviens des premiers moments où ma main a parcouru ce sanctuaire de feu; il m'a semblé trouver quelque chose de plus intime que sa nuque, et cette odeur de brûlé que j'aimais tant dans les cheveux. Je caressais tout son corps. J'essayais de me rapprocher le plus près possible de cet animal puissant qui attirait mon âme; il n'est pas un lieu de cette île que je ne voulais pas embrasser. C'était la magie de l'île magique: maintenant que je l'avais abordée, je ne pouvais plus m'en détacher. Il fallait plutôt que je m'y perde. Je ne pouvais plus repartir; je m'enfonçais le plus loin possible au fond des terres. Des voix m'appelaient . . . C'est un matin comme celui-là que la magie la plus inespérée m'enchaîna à ces rivages brûlants. Je l'avais dévêtue. Je sentais l'imminence d'un évènement qui pourtant me bouleversait trop. Je ne sais plus comment cela s'est produit. J'entrais en elle. Silencieusement. Elle était douce et mouvante, mon corps mouillé glissait dans son ventre, je sondais les parois de cette chapelle ardente, j'emplissais ces lieux sacrés de ma force et de mon plaisir. C'était une voûte de cathédrale qu'emplissait mon chant et l'écho me

the morning. We had distanced ourselves during the night without meaning to, and then when daylight came through the window, I turned again toward her and awakened her. She didn't even open her eyes. She complained a little because I displaced her. Her breasts were even warmer in the morning, and her back especially. I leaned on this strange balcony that she has at her flanks and there I stayed hanging for hours like one in despair. I kissed her belly. I clung to that mountain as though vertigo had seized me and I was afraid of falling into the void. I sank my hands into that rock scorched by the sun and I moistened her belly with my saliva. Every so often I grazed that black forest, that noble vegetation, that mane wilder than hair. I remember the first moments when my hand wandered through that sanctuary of fire; I seemed to have found something more intimate than the nape of her neck, and that smell of burning that I so loved in her hair. I caressed her whole body. I tried to bring myself as close as possible to that powerful animal that was attracting my soul; there was not one place on this isle that I did not want to kiss. It was the magic of the magic isle; now that I had reached it, I could no longer break loose. Instead I had to lose myself there. I could no longer set out again; I sank as far as possible into the depths of the earth. Voices called me . . . On a morning like that one the most unhoped for magic fettered me to those burning shores. I had undressed her. I felt the imminence of an event that nevertheless overwhelmed me too much. I no longer know how this came about. I entered her. Silently. She was gentle and shifting, my moistened body slipped into her belly, I sounded the walls of that candle-lit funeral chapel, I filled those sacred places with my strength and my pleasure. It was a cathedral vault that my chant filled, and the echo came back to me

revenait en même temps. Il n'est pas un repli que ma voix n'atteignait pas, pas une épaule que mon corps dilaté ne remplissait. Je connus cet instant où tout le corps se sent tiré par le dedans, où toute sa chaleur se ramasse en une seule plaie brûlante . . .

Je me roule dans mon lit. Ah il est pénible de se rappeler; j'ai le sentiment que mes souvenirs ne sont pas normaux. Il y manque toujours quelque chose. Que s'est-il passé exactement ce matin-là? Nous avons pourtant . . . Je ne suis plus sûr de ce qui revient à mon esprit. C'est idiot, je ne peux tout de même pas douter de cela. J'ai bien senti cet indiscutable arrachement dans le ventre qui est l'extase. J'ai bien connu cet essoufflement, et Hélène s'est bien tordue sous moi, il me semble. C'est bien son haleine que je recevais, et son bassin que je tenais de mes mains. Que manque-t-il à tout cela? Je souffre comme si je n'avais pas vécu ces instants et que je les désirasse affreusement. Tout semble s'échapper de moi. J'essaie de garder l'odeur âcre de son corps et le parfum grisant de son ventre. J'essaie de garder le poids de ses seins nus, mais tout glisse, il reste du sable. Que m'a-t-elle dit ce matin-là quand nous nous sommes séparés? Quand nous étions encore au lit peut-être? . . . Nous n'avons rien dit. Après non plus. J'ai fait chauffer l'eau pour le café, je suis allé chercher du pain. Je suis même retourné parce qu'il manquait de café. Quand je suis rentré, elle était habillée. C'était comme si rien ne s'était passé. Elle était peignée, propre, prête à partir. Elle était comme je l'avais vue cent fois avant: vêtue en noir, avec ce sourire ininterprétable et cet air immobile qui m'a décontenancé. Après la nuit que nous venions de passer, j'aurais voulu que nos propos soient plus secrets, plein de douces allusions. Mais non; nous avons parlé de je ne sais plus quoi. Deux personnes

at the same time. There was not an innermost recess that my voice did not reach, not a luff of the sail that my dilated body did not rejoice in filling. I knew that moment where the entire body feels itself turned inside out, where all its warmth gathers itself in a single burning wound . . .

I toss in my bed. Oh it is painful to recall; I have the feeling that my memories are not normal. There is always something missing. Exactly what happened that morning? We had nevertheless . . . I am no longer sure what I remember. It's crazy, all the same, I cannot doubt that. I certainly felt that unquestionable wrench in the belly that is ecstasy. I certainly was aware of that panting, and it seems to me Hélène certainly writhed beneath me. It is certainly her breath that I inhaled, and her pelvis that I held with my hands. What is lacking in all that? I suffer as though I had not lived those moments and were desiring them terribly. Everything seems to escape me. I try to preserve the pungent odour of her body and the intoxicating perfume of her belly. I try to preserve the weight of her naked breasts, but everything slips, what remains is sand. What did she say to me that morning when we parted? When we were still in bed, perhaps? . . . We said nothing. Afterwards neither. I heated water for coffee, I went to get bread. I even went back because there wasn't any coffee. When I came back, she was dressed. It was as though nothing had happened. Her hair was combed, she was clean and ready to leave. She was as I had seen her a hundred times before: dressed in black, with that uninterpretable smile and that motionless appearance that disconcerted me. After the night that we had just spent, I would have wanted our talk to be more secret, filled with sweet hints. But no, I no longer know what we spoke of. Two

prenant leur petit déjeuner ensemble, voilà de quoi nous avions l'air. Deux inconnus, deux amis. Nous avions pourtant passé la nuit dans le même lit. Oui, mais pas un mot, pas un seul mot dont je puisse me souvenir maintenant, pas une seule parole qui me revienne. Pas un seul aveu pour me prouver que je ne me trompe pas. Cherchons tout de même: elle a sûrement dit un mot à un certain moment, échappé une exclamation. A-t-elle murmuré mon nom? Même pas. Elle n'a pas échappé un cri . . . C'est impossible. Elle a sûrement parlé. Oui. L'heure. Elle a demandé l'heure. Et j'ai pris sa montre sur la table pour lui dire. C'est ridicule. Impossible de trouver une seule parole pour confirmer mes souvenirs. Un seul mot d'amour, un seul. Elle ne parle jamais, je sais. Oui, elle parle comme tout le monde, mais à un certain moment elle ne dit plus rien. Tout se fait en silence. Elle a une façon de passer brusquement à l'action. On arrête de parler. On ferme la lumière et l'étreinte se déroule. Pas un mot après, même soupiré. Pas une plainte avec mon nom au bout. Pas même la plainte toute seule qui vaudrait bien tous les aveux du monde. Pas même ce cri qu'arrache l'instant suprême. Elle retient son souffle. Même son haleine ne veut pas avouer, mais moi je sais, j'entends le bruit. Mais cela ne suffit pas. Il faudrait quelques paroles au moins, quelques mots qui prouvent que nous avons couché ensemble. C'est peut-être de ma faute ce silence idiot. La prochaine fois je lui arracherai un aveu; il faudra qu'elle me donne un mot. Je lui ferai trouver quelque chose de tendre à me dire, une chose secrète qu'on avoue seulement dans les situations extrêmes. Sinon, je lui arracherai un cri; j'irai fort, je ferai exprès. Je passerai la main très longtemps sans répit. Je n'arrêterai pas avant qu'elle ait parlé. Elle le poussera son soupir. Il y a des instants

people eating their breakfast together, that is what we looked like. Two unacquainted persons, two friends. Yet we had spent the night in the same bed. Yes, but not a word, not a single word that I can remember now, not a single exchange that comes back to me. Not a single acknowledgment to prove to myself that I am not mistaken. Let's think all the same: surely she spoke a word at a certain moment, let slip an exclamation. Did she murmur my name? Not even that. She didn't let slip a cry . . . That's impossible. Surely she spoke. Yes. The time. She asked the time. And I took her watch from the table to tell her. That's ridiculous. Impossible to find a single exchange to confirm my memories. A single word of love, only one. She never speaks, I know. Yes, she speaks like everyone, but at a certain moment she no longer says anything. All is done in silence. She has a way of passing abruptly into action. We stop talking. We turn off the light and the embracing begins. Not a word afterward, even sighed. Not a moan with my name at the end. Not even the moan that by itself certainly would be worth all the open declarations in the world. Not even that cry brought forth by the supreme moment. She holds her breath. Even her breathing does not want to make a declaration, but I know, I hear the sound. But that is not enough. There must be some talk at least, some words that prove that we have slept together. Maybe this absurd silence is my fault. The next time I will extract an acknowledgment from her; she will have to speak a word to me. I will make her find something tender to say to me, something secret that we utter only in extreme situations. If not, I will extract a cry from her; I'll go at it hard, I'll do it on purpose. I'll use my hand for a very long time without stopping. I won't stop until she has spoken. She will heave that sigh of hers. There are

où l'on ne retient pas sa respiration. Je ferai palpiter ce ventre jusqu'à ce qu'il en sorte une parole. Alors seulement je la comblerai. Elle ne sait pas ce que c'est que l'incertitude et l'éloignement. Près, il y a toujours le corps qui peut remplacer à tout moment toutes les certitudes du monde. Mais loin, perdu dans une chambre au fond de la via Giuseppe Barilli à Naples, il faut d'autres certitudes. Car le corps même devient incertain et nos souvenirs improbables. Il me faudrait une parole pour croire que j'ai vraiment touché ses cuisses, embrassé sa poitrine, pénétré de toute mon âme au fond de son gouffre noir... Les souvenirs sont tellement vagues. Et comment sentir la chaleur d'un corps si je ne le touche plus.

∞

Je ne savais pas que le temps pouvait être si long. Je marche, et il ne se passe rien. Il fait toujours soleil. C'est l'époque de l'année où les jours sont le plus longs. Je commence à avoir les jambes raides. Je m'asseois à une terrasse, mais je ne reste jamais plus d'une demi-heure au même endroit. Je repars. Dix minutes après, je suis encore fatigué et je m'asseois. Il faut attendre un peu avant de repartir. J'essaie de le mériter. Quand j'enfile une rue, je regarde tout de suite jusqu'au bout si je ne distingue pas une annonce de café. Je n'ai même pas le goût d'aller au musée. On me montrerait le plus grand chef d'oeuvre de la terre que je dirais: une autre fois, demain. On me dirait: marchez encore cinq minutes et vous rencontrerez Dieu en personne, que je dirais: tant pis, je m'asseois. Mon septième café depuis le matin: j'étends les jambes et je regarde. Le monde finit ici. Allez dire à la Joconde et à Dieu de défiler devant moi, je les regarderai volontiers. Il y a assez

moments where you don't hold your breath. I will make that belly rise and fall until a word comes out. Only then will I satisfy her. She doesn't know what uncertainty and distance are. Close by, there is always the body that at every moment can replace all the certainties of the world. But far away, lost in a room at the bottom of Via Giuseppe Barilli in Naples, other certainties are necessary. Because even the body becomes uncertain and our memories improbable. I need a word to believe that I truly touched her thighs, kissed her bosom, penetrated with all my soul to the depths of her black abyss . . . My memories are so vague. And how can I feel the warmth of a body if I'm no longer touching it.

∞

I didn't know that time could pass so slowly. I walk, and nothing happens. It stays sunny. It's the time of year when the days are the longest. My legs are beginning to get stiff. I sit down at a café, but I never stay longer than half an hour in the same spot. I start off again. Ten minutes later, I'm tired once more and I sit down. I have to wait a little before starting off again. I try to deserve it. When I turn a corner, I look right away to the end of the street to see if I can make out a sign for a café. I don't even feel like going to a museum. You could show me the greatest masterpiece on earth and I'd say: some other time, tomorrow. You could tell me, walk another five minutes and you'll see God in person, and I'd say: too bad, I'm sitting down. My seventh coffee since morning: I stretch out my legs and look around. The world ends here. Go tell the Mona Lisa and God to march past me, I'll readily look at them. There are enough

de ces Napolitains qui m'épuisent. À toutes les trois minutes, je tâte la poche de mon veston. C'est un préjugé de touriste, mais je ne saurais m'en débarasser. Quand j'aborde un Napolitain, je le regarde comme un ennemi. S'il approche, je me câbre. Je le traite intérieurement de sale Italien, de lâche, de voleur et je bénis le ciel de vivre dans le Nord. Parfois je les aime et j'ai le goût, comme eux, d'embrasser tout le monde. Quand je les entends chanter, je les aime. Je voudrais chanter comme eux à longueur de journée . . .

Marchons un peu maintenant. Tiens, si j'allais à la gare vérifier l'horaire. Non tout de même. J'ai tout vérifié cent fois. Elle arrive à 11.30 heures, c'est définitif. N'y pensons plus et marchons sans être troublé. Marcher, c'est tout ce qui me reste. Et regarder les visages. Les visages de femmes surtout. Ils sont admirablement reposés, des visages paresseux et comblés. Ces femmes doivent avoir des gestes merveilleux dans un lit. Le plaisir qu'on donne à un animal aussi spontané doit nous être remis au centuple et par tout ce que leur reconnaissance peut inventer, en retour, de douceur. Hélène n'a pas de ces gestes de reconnaissance animale. Elle ressemble à ces amis qui n'accusent jamais réception des cadeaux. Un an plus tard, ils vous annoncent que ça leur a procuré un grand plaisir. Je m'attends à une rétrospective du genre avec Hélène . . . Parlez-moi de ces vierges qui viennent vous chanter, quand tout est bien fini, qu'elles auraient voulu se faire violer. Il doit y avoir une façon de vivre au jour le jour sans accumuler du matériel à dévoilement posthume. Je n'ai pas le temps d'attendre la mort de mes amis pour savoir s'ils m'ont aimé. Et quand je tiens Hélène dans mes bras, je voudrais bien savoir si elle jouit. Elle devrait tomber dans les transes, vibrer de tout son corps, haleter, crier, se tordre comme un poisson qui se débat

of these Neapolitans who wear me out. Every three minutes, I feel the pocket of my jacket. It's the prejudice of a tourist, but I don't know how to shake it off. When I approach a Neapolitan, I view him as an enemy. If he comes near, I recoil. Inwardly I call him a dirty Italian, a coward, a thief, and I thank heaven that I live in the North. Sometimes I like them and I feel disposed, like them, to embrace everyone. When I hear them sing, I like them. I would like to sing as they do all day long . . .

Let's walk a little now. Hey, suppose I go to the station to check the schedule. Really, no. I've checked everything a hundred times. She arrives at 11:30, that's definite. Let's not think about it any more and let's walk without worrying. Walking, that's all that's left to me. And looking at faces. Especially the faces of women. They are wonderfully at ease, idle and satisfied faces. These women must have marvellous moves in a bed. The pleasure that is bestowed on such a natural animal should be given back a hundredfold and by all that their gratitude can devise, in return, of sweetness. Hélène does not have these moves of animal gratitude. She is like those friends who never acknowledge a gift. A year later, they declare that it brought them great pleasure. I'm expecting that kind of delayed reaction from Hélène . . . Tell me about these virgins who give you the line, when everything is all over, that they would rather have been raped. There must be a way of living from day to day without accumulating material for posthumous discovery. I don't have the time to wait for the death of my friends to know whether they loved me. And when I hold Hélène in my arms, I certainly would like to know if she comes. She should fall into trances, her whole body should quiver, she should pant, moan, and writhe like a fish that struggles

au bout de l'hameçon. Je ne connais pas de plus grande cruauté que l'économie des gestes, que les ventres qui refusent de palpiter au bon moment, que les mains qui n'osent s'agiter le long du dos. Le corps est fait pour cela: s'agiter dans le plaisir, se prostrer dans le chagrin, gémir dans la douleur. Il faudrait le dépouiller de cette fierté qui tient le cou raide quand il devrait se rompre. C'est ce que je détestais en Hélène: cette façon de ne jamais perdre contenance, de garder le buste tendu, la tête brandie comme une insulte. Le corps n'est pas un palais de marbre avec des colonnes immobiles et blanches, des voûtes éternelles . . . , mais une plante fébrile faite pour vibrer à tous les vents, s'épanouir au soleil du matin et mourir si une main distraite vient la déraciner. Je déteste les corps qui se prennent pour des châteaux et qui refusent d'éclater en mille morceaux au moment d'une grande joie. Je déteste ces murs opaques qui regardent les passants comme des voleurs ou des bandits, et les marbres immobiles dont on veut recouvrir cette vermine émouvante qu'est la chair. Quand je l'avais dans mes bras et que je l'avais blessée au ventre, j'aurais voulu que ces murs trop bien gardés se fendent, que ces portes de fer se déchirent et me laissent voir enfin un jardin plein de fraîcheur . . . J'aurais souhaité que tant de maladresse et tant de silence cachât quelque secret qui en valût la peine.

Mais cela en vaut la peine! Puisque j'ignore encore ce qui s'y trouve. J'ai beau me passer la tête à travers ces grilles si peu accueillantes, je n'y vois que de l'ombre, une noirceur insondable dont je ne puis détacher mon regard, une sorte d'espace vague où je puis imaginer les plus beaux jardins de la terre, des fleurs inconnues et des fontaines éternelles. Mais s'il n'y a que de la pierre au fond de ce palais maudit, si tout cela est en marbre, s'il n'y a pas de fleur

on the end of a hook. I don't know of a greater cruelty than paucity of gestures, than bellies that refuse to throb at the right moment, than hands that do not dare to stroke one's back. The body is made for that: to shake with pleasure, to prostrate itself in sorrow, to groan in pain. It must be stripped of that pride that holds the neck stiff when it should be breaking. That is what I hated about Hélène: that way of never losing composure, of keeping her torso tensed, her head brandished like an insult. The body is not a palace of marble with motionless white columns, eternal vaults . . . , but a feverish plant made to quiver in every wind, to blossom in the morning sun and die if a heedless hand comes to uproot it. I hate bodies that take themselves for castles and that refuse to explode into a thousand pieces at a moment of great joy. I hate these opaque walls that look at passers-by as if they were thieves or bandits, and the motionless marbles with which they want to overlay this thrilling riff-raff that is flesh. When I had her in my arms and I had wounded her in the belly, I would have wanted those overprotected walls to break apart, those gates of iron to tear and let me see at last a garden filled with freshness . . . I would have wished that so much awkwardness and so much silence had been hiding some secret that was worth the trouble.

But it is worth the trouble! Since I still know nothing about what is found there. Try as I might to get my head through these unwelcoming gratings, I see only shadow there, an unfathomable blackness from which I cannot turn my gaze, a sort of vague space where I can imagine the most beautiful gardens on earth, unknown flowers and eternal fountains. But if there is nothing but stone at the heart of this accursed palace, if everything is made of marble, if

qui respire dans cette prison, je détruirai tout cela. Je grifferai ces pierres prétentieuses jusqu'à ce qu'il n'en reste que poussière et sable.

Ce Napolitain qui gesticule devant la police : je veux qu'Hélène soit comme lui. Je veux que la moindre pensée s'exprime par quarante gestes du corps. Je veux que son front se brise, que ses yeux s'agrandissent, que son visage se déforme, que sa bouche trop délicate saigne et que son cou se rompe à la première émotion. Je veux qu'elle perde son identité quand je la touche et qu'elle meure quand je la possède . . .

∽

Encore toute une soirée devant ces fleurs. Une prison avec des fleurs sur les murs. Je suis cerné. Je ne peux regarder nulle part sans apercevoir ces pétales affreux. Ces fleurs ont été inventées par les tapissiers pour égayer les chambres d'hôtels, pour nous faire croire que les murs ont des germes, qu'ils sont peuplés de petites bêtes et de racines et que tout cela pousse pour le bon plaisir du voyageur. Toute la soirée et toute la nuit dans ce jardin écoeurant, à respirer le parfum de mes fleurs. Attendons patiemment demain matin. Demain matin. Tiens ça me réchauffe. L'instant où je l'apercevrai sur le quai. Elle aura son costume noir probablement. Je l'aime, en noir. Quand je pense à elle, elle m'apparaît toujours en noir. Je la vois apparaître sur le bord du quai. Elle ne me voit pas encore. Moi, je suis à la grille de la sortie. Elle avance vers moi. J'aime la regarder marcher seule. Elle fait de grands pas, pas très féminins je sais. Mais il y a tellement de vigueur dans cette démarche. Un temps, je me moquais de

there is no flower that breathes in this prison, I will destroy it all. I'll claw at these pretentious stones until nothing remains but dust and sand.

This Neapolitan who is making gestures in front of the police: I want Hélène to be like him. I want the slightest thought to express itself in forty movements of the body. I want her forehead to shatter, her eyes to grow wide, her face to distort, her too-delicate mouth to bleed, and her neck to break at the first sign of emotion. I want her to lose her identity when I touch her, and to die when I possess her . . .

☙

Another whole evening in front of these flowers. A prison with flowers on the walls. I am surrounded. I can't look anywhere without seeing these frightful petals. These flowers were contrived by decorators to brighten hotel rooms, to make us believe that the walls have seeds, that they are filled with little animals and roots, and that it all grows for the enjoyment of the traveller. All evening and all night in this loathsome garden, breathing the perfume of my flowers. Let's wait patiently for tomorrow morning. Tomorrow morning. Hey, that perks me up. The moment when I will see her on the platform. She probably will have her black dress on. I love her in black. When I think of her, she always appears in black. I see her appear on the edge of the platform. She doesn't see me yet. Me, I'm at the grating of the exit gate. She advances toward me. I love to watch her walking alone. She takes large steps, not very feminine, I know. But there is such vigour in that gait. Once, I made fun of her way of

sa façon de marcher; je trouvais qu'elle marchait comme un joueur de tennis. Elle pose le pied légèrement en dedans. Je la reconnaîtrais à un mille: sa tête droite, ses épaules immobiles et ce balancement merveilleux, ce rythme puissant des cuisses et des hanches. Est-ce qu'elle me voit? Je lui fais signe. Elle ne m'a pas encore aperçu. Je l'appelle, elle s'approche de moi. Elle me sourit en approchant, plus vivement que d'habitude. Son visage est plus éclairé. C'est la joie d'arriver sans doute. Rarement elle a eu cette expression: il y a toujours du clair obscur dans ses traits, comme si la lumière ne frappait qu'en un seul endroit à la fois. Je surprends l'éclat de ses yeux, mais la bouche est étrange, ses lèvres restent sinueuses . . . Mais cette fois, tout est illuminé. L'obscur est à côté d'elle, c'est ce qui l'entoure. Moi je ne vois que ce visage rayonnant et magiquement éclairé. Je l'embrasse. Je l'ai prise fortement, son corps s'est frappé au mien, puis je pose mes lèvres sur les siennes. Je cherche ce point de douceur, cette couche de salive où tremper mon âme asséchée. C'est une fontaine que j'effleure et qui me rend la vie . . . Je ne l'embrasse pas longtemps, car elle a des choses à raconter: son voyage, quand il lui a fallu changer de voiture, ses embêtements à la gare de Rome . . .

∞

J'étais debout un soir chez elle, prêt à partir. Il devait être assez tard. Je n'avais rien fait de la soirée. Nous en étions restés à parler théâtre et cinéma, ce qui devient vite exaspérant car on finit par ne plus savoir ce qu'on dit. Je me moquais des opinions que je lançais: j'observais ses jambes, ses genoux découverts, son cou, ses bras. J'aurais pu affirmer le contraire de tout ce que je disais, cela m'était vraiment indifférent.

walking; I thought she was walking like a tennis player. She turns her foot in slightly. I would recognize her a mile away: her head held high, her shoulders motionless and that marvellous balance, that powerful rhythm of thighs and hips. Does she see me? I wave at her. She hasn't noticed me yet. I call to her, she comes toward me. She smiles at me as she approaches, with more life than usual. Her face is lit up. No doubt it's the joy of arrival. Rarely has she had this expression: there is always chiaroscuro in her features, as though the light only struck one spot at a time. I catch the flash in her eyes, but her mouth is odd, her lips remain twisted . . . But this time, everything is lighted. The darkness is beside her, it is what surrounds her. Me, I only see this radiant and magically illuminated face. I kiss her. I held her tight, her body struck mine, then I put my lips on hers. I seek this place of sweetness, this bed of saliva where my dried out soul can soak. It is a fountain that I skim and which restores life to me . . . I don't kiss her for long, because she has things to tell: her journey, when she had to change coaches, her problems at the station in Rome . . .

∞

One evening I was standing at her place, ready to leave. It must have been fairly late. I had done nothing all evening. We never got past talking about theatre and film, which quickly became exasperating because you end up by no longer knowing what you've said. I made fun of the opinions that I tossed out: I watched her legs, her uncovered knees, her neck, her arms. I could have asserted the opposite of everything I said, it really made no difference to me. She must have

Elle devait comprendre d'ailleurs qu'autre chose m'occupait. Puis, je me suis levé pour partir. Il y eut un silence prolongé. Nous avions quitté la veine du bavardage; ce silence abolissait d'un coup la surcharge de mots qui avaient précédé. Je la regardais en me disant: cette soirée est perdue. J'y étais presque résigné. J'ouvris la porte. Hélène ne disait pas un mot. Souriait-elle, je ne sais plus. Je ressentis alors une telle colère devant la privation qui me brûlait. J'entrevoyais le retour à la maison et ma rage de n'avoir pas touché ce corps merveilleux, de n'avoir rien fait pour apaiser le plus impérieux de mes désirs. Je refermai la porte et me tournai vers elle. Je la pris par les épaules et l'attirai à moi. Je la serrais très fort, je l'aurais griffé tellement cette étreinte me calmait. Je l'embrassai. J'avais le sentiment de retrouver un paradis que ma folie m'aurait fait perdre. La fraîcheur de ses lèvres sur les miennes rachetait les paroles inutiles de toute la soirée. Elle se plaça un peu mieux sous mon épaule et là, debout contre ce mur, nous nous sommes embrassés profondément. Je passais ma langue sous la sienne, je caressais ce lieu tendre du mieux que je pouvais. Nous sommes restés longtemps à respirer nos haleines. Je ne pensais même pas à nous jeter sur le lit juste à côté, car il eût fallu déranger cette harmonie si précaire, et qui sait si jamais nos bouches se seraient unies avec un tel bonheur une fois sur le lit? Peut-être n'auraient-elles jamais retrouvé cet accord, cette sensation de dire adieu sur le bord d'un précipice, ce sentiment qu'un baiser est aussi fragile et aussi précieux que le temps qui fuit? C'est ainsi que je vois la vie: une suite d'instants privilégiés arrachés à l'imprévisible. Celui qui sent constamment sur sa nuque la présence d'une main glacée sait que le moindre instant est irréversible, que

understood anyway that something else was on my mind. Then I got up to leave. There was a prolonged silence. We had stopped our stream of chattering; this silence put a sudden end to the excess of words that had preceded. I looked at her, saying to myself: this evening is lost. I had almost given up. I opened the door. Hélène didn't say a word. Was she smiling, I no longer know. Then I felt such an anger from the deprivation burning in me. I anticipated going home and foresaw my rage at not having touched that marvellous body, at having done nothing to appease my most pressing desire. I closed the door again and turned toward her. I took her by the shoulders and drew her to me. I squeezed her very hard. I would have scratched her body, so much did this embrace calm me. I kissed her. I had the feeling of regaining a paradise that my madness would have caused me to lose. The freshness of her lips on mine redeemed the useless talk of the whole evening. She positioned herself a little better under my shoulder, and there, standing against that wall, we kissed one another passionately. I slipped my tongue under hers, I caressed that tender spot as well as I could. We spent a long time taking in each other's breaths. I didn't even think of throwing ourselves onto the bed right beside us, because it would have meant disturbing such a precarious harmony, and who knows if our mouths would have ever been united with such bliss once on the bed? Perhaps they would never have regained that accord, that feeling of saying goodbye on the edge of a precipice, that feeling that a kiss is as fragile and precious as time that flees? That is how I see life: a succession of privileged moments wrenched from the unforeseeable. He who constantly feels the presence of an icy hand at the nape of his neck knows that the briefest moment is irreversible, that the

le baiser précaire c'est toujours ça de pris sur la mort. Ceux qui ont besoin d'être bien placés pour s'aimer, ceux qui requièrent des chandelles, la pleine lune et la musique tzigane pour entreprendre le rituel, je les plains. La grâce ne vient pas toucher l'homme seulement quand il est assis et qu'il a bien digéré. L'amour est comme le célèbre voleur de l'évangile. Si c'est dans l'endroit le moins indiqué et le plus mal choisi que ce feu s'empare de deux mortels, c'est là précisément qu'ils trouveront leur instant suprême, et pas ailleurs. Debout contre une grille froide, sur un coin de rue en plein hiver, dans un lit sale ils toucheront le ciel. Cet instant sans prétention est leur éternité. L'éternité pour moi c'est de posséder Hélène. C'est une sorte de passerelle au-dessus du vide et qui d'un moment à l'autre peut craquer. Nous sommes suspendus à ce pont créé par nos lèvres et nos corps qui se joignent. Nous nous sommes rencontrés en pleine noirceur et sur la frange du néant; à peine avions-nous le temps de nous regarder entre deux étreintes. Nous sommes des complices: nous nous connaissons mal, nous ne disons pas un mot, nous sommes précipités dans une action trop rapide pour nous. Nous nous unissons contre le noir et nous mourrons ensemble peut-être, mais sans nous être connus. J'ai oublié ton visage: je me souviens de la fraîcheur de ta bouche et du goût de ton haleine le matin à sept heures. Tu as peut-être quelque détail sur ton visage qui te distingue? Tes yeux sont-ils cernés? Tes paupières, comment sont-elles? Je connais la chaleur de tes joues, mais je ne saurais retrouver leur dessin. Ton front est fier, mais où commencent les cheveux. J'ai oublié tout cela. Il devait faire noir quand nous nous sommes connus, car j'ai oublié ton visage. Je me souviens de l'odeur de ton corps et du poids de ton ventre et de la chaleur de tes seins.

precarious kiss is always something snatched from death. Those who need the right circumstances to make love, those who require candles, the full moon and gypsy music to engage in the ritual, those I pity. Grace does not come to touch a man only when he is seated and has properly digested. Love is like the celebrated thief of the gospel. If it is in the least likely and worst chosen place that this fire takes possession of two mortals, it is precisely there that they will find their supreme moment, and not elsewhere. Standing against a cold grating, on a street corner in the depths of winter, in a soiled bed they will touch heaven. This moment without pretense is their eternity. Eternity for me is to possess Hélène. It is a sort of footbridge over the void and which from one moment to the next can give way. We are suspended on this bridge created by our lips and our bodies that are joined to one another. We met in complete darkness and on the fringe of nothingness; we scarcely had time to exchange glances between two embraces. We are confederates: we hardly know each other, we don't say a word, we are pushed headlong into an act too rushed for us. We are united against the darkness and perhaps we will die together, but without having known each other. I have forgotten your face: I remember the freshness of your mouth and the taste of your breath at seven in the morning. Do you have perhaps some detail on your face that distinguishes you? Do you have circles under your eyes? Your eyelids, what are they like? I recognize the warmth of your cheeks, but I wouldn't know how to draw them. Your forehead is noble, but where does your hair begin? I have forgotten all that. It must have been dark when we got to know each other, because I have forgotten your face. I remember the smell of your body and the weight of your belly and the warmth of your

Toi, te souviens-tu de moi ? Sais-tu comment est faite ma lèvre aux commissures, comment sont dispersés mes sourcils ? Pourrais-tu dire seulement si j'ai des cheveux gris ? Tu ne les a peut-être pas vus, mais j'en ai sur les tempes, sur le dessus de la tête, en avant même . . .

Nous avons scellé un pacte en pleine nuit parce qu'il faisait froid, que nous étions pressés et que nous ne pouvions plus attendre . . . Ce sera drôle de nous revoir demain. Tout sera à recommencer. D'ailleurs, le jour, nous sommes gênés ensemble. Nous ne savons pas de quoi parler : c'est comme si on venait de nous présenter l'un à l'autre et qu'il fallait, par contenance, ne pas laisser tomber la conversation. Nous ne serons jamais à l'aise quand nous prendrons le métro ensemble, quand nous ferons la queue au cinéma, ou que nous nous rencontrerons par hasard sur la rue en plein après-midi . . . Nous serons toujours des étrangers, le jour. Mais quand la nuit tombe sur nos deux corps, nous nous reconnaissons ; quand nos ventres se rapprochent, notre véritable intimité se révèle. Alors, nous savons pourquoi nous sommes ensemble, nous n'avons plus de comédie à jouer. C'est au fond d'un lit sombre, palpitant de rage et de plaisir, que nous sommes le plus profondément unis. Nous sommes unis contre la mort : c'est là toute notre intimité. Le reste, ce bavardage sur les trottoirs, à la porte des cinémas, ce sont des amoindrissements. Notre pacte n'admet pas ces mensonges : nous sommes des complices contre la mort et il n'y a pas dix façons de conjurer la mort, mais une seule. Une seule chaleur pour combattre le froid, une seule rage contre le néant, une seule volupté contre l'ennui. Voilà pourquoi nous sommes unis, mais si tragiquement que nous n'aurons jamais le temps de nous connaître . . .

C'est le soleil. Il est dix heures et demie ! Mais comment se fait-il que j'aie tant dormi. Je suis tout en nage maintenant . . . C'était affreux. J'essayais de la prendre et je me luttais à cette chose invisible. Quel

breasts. You, do you remember me? Do you know how my lip curves at the corners of my mouth, how my eyebrows are spread? Could you even say if I have grey hair? Perhaps you haven't seen it, but I have some at the temples, on the top of my head, even in front . . .

We sealed a pact in the middle of the night because it was cold, that we were in a hurry and that we couldn't wait any longer . . . It will be funny to see each other tomorrow. We will have to start all over again. Besides, in the daytime, we are awkward together. We don't know what to talk about: it's as though we had just met and it was necessary, for the sake of form, not to let the conversation die. We will never be at ease when we take the metro together, when we stand in line at the movies, or if we meet by chance on the street in the middle of the afternoon . . . We will always be strangers by day. But when night falls on our two bodies, we recognize each other; when our bellies draw together, our true intimacy reveals itself. Then we know why we are together; we no longer have to put on an act. It is down on a dark bed, throbbing with fury and pleasure, that we are most profoundly united. We are united against death: there is the sum of our intimacy. The rest, this chatting on sidewalks, at the entrance to movie theatres, these are diminutions. Our pact does not allow for lies: we are confederates against death, and there are not ten ways to stave off death, but only one. Only one warmth to combat the cold, only one rage against nothingness, only one sensual delight against tedium. That is why we are united, but so tragically that we will never have the time to get to know each other . . .

It's sunny. It's ten thirty! But how did it happen that I slept so much. I'm drenched in sweat now . . . It was dreadful. I was trying to take hold of her and I was struggling with this invisible thing.

rêve. Elle était derrière une vitre et moi je me frappais contre, j'avais le visage en sang. Toujours cette vitre qui ne se brisait pas... Heureusement qu'il y a la réalité parfois. Il me reste encore une chemise propre, je l'ai gardée spécialement pour ce matin. Où l'ai-je placée. Ah oui, la petite valise... Je me frappais contre cette vitre, mais ce qui me désespérait, c'est qu'Hélène ne me voyait pas. La vitre était pourtant transparente. Hélène ne semblait pas entendre le bruit que je faisais. Elle souriait légèrement, mais pas vers moi. Je criais, je frappais, elle ne me voyait même pas à travers cette glace translucide comme le jour. Je me déchirais pour qu'elle me regarde et elle ne s'apercevait pas de moi. Elle souriait comme ce matin-là quand je revins avec le pain et le café pour le petit déjeuner. Une glace entre ce sourire et moi. Je perdais tout mon sang et je la regardais sourire... *Perdonate signor, ma que vettura besugno prendere per andare à la stazione?* — "Vous partir? *Un momento... il conto è non preparato*" — Mais non je ne pars pas... *Io va... rencontrare une personna à la stazione* — "*Partire oggi o domani?*" — *Oggi, ma non adesso, questa sera* — "*Va bene*" — *Io volio scire questa vettura...* — "*Per la stazione?... numero otto*" — Merci. Andouille. Il ne comprend jamais rien. *Numero otto,* où est-ce qu'il se promène lui? Je devrais prendre un petit café avant de me rendre à la gare. Tant pis, voici mon tramway. Il fait chaud là-dedans, et quelle cargaison... Gesticulez, mais ne me touchez pas, s'il vous plaît. Hélène doit avoir passé Formia en ce moment. Elle doit plutôt approcher d'Aversa. Elle aperçoit peut-être la baie de Naples... *Uno per la stazione, prego* — "*Vinticinque lire*" — *Momento,* on va te payer si seulement je peux glisser ma main dans mon gousset. Je n'ai plus de petite monnaie. Quelle tête fera-t-il maintenant si je lui présente un mille.

What a dream. She was behind a pane of glass while I was throwing myself against it, my face was bloody. Always this glass that wouldn't break . . . Fortunately there is reality at times. I still have a clean shirt, I kept it especially for this morning. Where did I put it? Oh yes, the small suitcase . . . I was throwing myself against this pane of glass, but what distressed me was that Hélène didn't see me. However, the glass was transparent. Hélène did not seem to hear the noise that I was making. She smiled slightly, but not toward me. I shouted, I hammered, she didn't even see me through that cold plate glass as translucent as daylight. I was tearing myself to pieces to get her to look at me and she didn't notice me. She was smiling like that morning when I came back with bread and coffee for breakfast. Cold plate glass between that smile and me. I was losing all my blood and I watched her smiling . . . *Perdonate signor, ma que vettura besugno prendere per andare à la stazione?* — "You want to go? *Un momento . . . il conto è non preparato*" — But no, I'm not leaving . . . *Io va . . . rencontrare une personna à la stazione* — "*Partire oggi o domani?*" — *Oggi, ma non adesso, quest sera* — "*Va bene*" — *Io volio scire questa vettura . . .* — "*Per la stazione? . . . numero otto*" — Thanks. Goof. He never understands anything. *Numero otto,* where is he off to? I should grab a quick coffee before getting to the station. Too bad, here's my streetcar. It's hot inside, and what a cargo . . . Wave your arms around, but don't touch me, please. Hélène must have passed Formia by now. Rather, she must be getting near Aversa. Perhaps she can see the bay of Naples . . . *Uno per la stazione, prego* — "*Vinticinque lire*" — *Momento,* you'll get paid if I can just slip my hand into my watch pocket. I don't have any more small change. What fuss is he going to make now if I give him a thousand. But I

SHIFTING SANDS / 47

Mais, je n'ai qu'un cinq mille! Tant pis. — *"Cinquemille! Cinquemille lire per la stazione? Perche non dieci mille per un passagerio da vinti lire? Qui è non il direttissimo per Roma, ma solamento un piccolo trammino e costa vinticinque lire, vinticinque italiane lire, vinticinque republicane lire . . ."* — Qu'est-ce que je vais répondre à cet énergumène? Moi je veux tout juste me rendre à la gare. Je m'en fous pas mal de la republique. *Scusate, ma ho niente monneta* . . . Qu'est-ce qu'il raconte maintenant. Cette fois je ne comprends rien. Et ces badauds qui me regardent parce que je n'ai pas de monnaie. Tiens regardez là, un beau cinq mille. Ce n'est tout de même pas de ma faute si votre pays en fabrique de ces machins-là . . . Bon, c'est le coup de l'étranger. Ils le savent maintenant. — "Cher monsieur, je comprends votre situation, j'ai longtemps vécu en France . . ." — Mais pourquoi donne-t-il 25 lires au conducteur? — "Je vous prie monsieur laissez faire" — Le conducteur prend la monnaie et remet un billet au type. Mais je ne peux pas accepter. C'est ridicule. Les autres me regardent avec le sourire maintenant. Remercions ce francophile. Tout le tramway me regarde. Moi j'ai l'air d'un bel imbécile. Attendons cette maudite gare. Qu'est-ce qu'ils ont tous à me regarder comme si j'avais une tache sur la joue ou un col mal fait? C'est long pour la gare . . . *"Stazione centrale!"* — *Scendo qui,* io scendo qui. La sortie maintenant. Il est 11 heures et dix. Trente minutes seulement et le train sera là. *Dove è l'uscita?* Il doit y avoir des billets de quai . . . Pas de monnaie? Trouvez-en de la monnaie. Je suis pressé, moi. Si on manque de monnaie dans les gares maintenant, où allons-nous? Qu'est-ce qu'il peut bien raconter lui? Aller aux guichets? Mais où les guichets? Je vous dis que je suis pressé, j'attends quelqu'un sur le train de Rome. Comprenez-vous? Il est bouché! Laissez-moi passer quand même. Vous voyez bien que je

only have a five thousand! Too bad. — *"Cinquemille! Cinquemille lire per la stazione? Perche non dieci mille per un passagerio da vinti lire? Qui è non il direttissimo per Roma, ma solamento un piccolo trammino et costa vinticinque lire, vinticinque italiane lire, vinticinque republicane lire . . ."* — What am I going to say to this ranter? All I want is to get to the station. I could give a flying fuck for the republic. *Scusate, ma ho niente monnetta . . .* What is he going on about now. This time I don't understand anything. And these gawkers who look at me because I have no change. Here, take a look at that, a nice five thousand. After all, it's not my fault if your country produces those whatchamacallits . . . Good, that's the blowoff of the foreigner. Now they know it. — "Dear sir, I understand your situation, I lived in France for a long time . . ." — But why is he giving 25 lire to the conductor? — "I beg you sir, let me take care of this" — The conductor takes the change and gives a ticket to the guy. But I can't accept. It's ridiculous. The others are smiling at me now. Let's thank this francophile. The whole streetcar is looking at me. I'm coming across like a total idiot. Let's wait for this damned station. What's with them all looking at me as though I have a spot on my cheek or a messed up collar? It's so far to the station . . . *"Stazione centrale!"* — *Scendo qui, io scendo qui.* Now the exit. It's eleven-ten. Just thirty minutes and the train will be there. *Dove è l'uscita?* There must be platform tickets . . . No change? Find some change. Look, I'm in a hurry. If you can't get change in the stations now, where do you go? What is that guy saying? Go to the ticket windows? But where are the ticket windows? I tell you I'm in a hurry, I'm expecting someone on the train from Rome. Do you understand? Is he ever dense! Let me get by anyway. You can plainly see that I only

n'ai qu'un 5000. — *"Aspete qui, farniente"* — Laissez-moi passer, ce sera beaucoup plus simple. Un train arrive. *Questo . . . , da Roma?* C'est celui-là. Elle doit passer ici tout de même, je la verrai. — *"Direttissimo provenienza da Roma è arrivato al binario novedieci"* — Il en descend du monde de ce train . . . Non . . . , non . . . , non . . . , pas elle, non . . . C'est normal. Elle ne descend pas tout de suite, elle a trop de baggages . . . Une femme ! . . . non. Cette grille est embêtante. Ceux qui sortent passent devant moi et m'empêchent de voir. Plusieurs femmes tout d'un coup. Non pas elle, non . . . , pas elle non plus. En noir, les cheveux courts, une seule valise, sa démarche . . . non. Hélène est plus grande que ça: elle n'a pas ce visage d'ailleurs. Une autre encore, non . . . , non . . . C'est fatiguant de regarder à travers cette grille. Il faut toujours calculer entre deux barreaux, et à distance. Je devrais regarder ceux qui sortent de côté pour être sûr. Inutile, c'est elle. Je la vois. Les groupes sont de plus en plus denses maintenant. Cela me rassure. Plus il y en a qui sortent du train, plus je suis rassuré. Elle doit approcher. Une femme en noir, avec deux valises. Elle s'avance vers moi. Non, ce n'est pas Hélène. Une autre: elle marche comme Hélène. Non tout de même, Hélène marche plus élégamment. Puis, elle ne porte jamais de talons hauts. Rarement. Parfois tout de même. J'ai de la difficulté à discerner les démarches maintenant. En fait, je ne sais plus comment marche Hélène. Est-ce qu'elle porte les épaules en avant ? Il me semble que non. Elle ne se balance pas en tout cas; elle reste droite. Il ne vient presque plus personne maintenant. Elle a probablement du trouble avec ses valises. Ou peut-être croit-elle que je vais l'attendre sur le quai ? Elle a bien pris ce train, j'espère . . . Oui sûrement. On ne peut pas se tromper de train. Voici un porteur, elle doit le suivre. Elle est trop fatiguée pour porter ses baggages elle-même. Non, ce n'est pas elle . . . Mais enfin. C'est

have a 5000. — *"Aspete qui, farniente"* — Let me go through, that will be a lot simpler. A train is arriving. *Questo . . . , da Roma?* It's that one there. She has to go by here anyway, I will see her. — *"Direttissimo provenienza da Roma è arrivato al binario novedieci"* — A lot of people are getting off this train . . . No . . . , no . . . , no . . . , not her, no . . . That's usual. She isn't getting off right away, she has too much luggage . . . A woman! . . . no. This grating is annoying. Those who are going out pass in front of me and keep me from seeing. Several women all at once. Not her, no . . . , not her either. In black, hair short, only one suitcase, her gait . . . no. Hélène is taller than that: she doesn't look like that either. Yet another one, no . . . , no . . . It's tiring to look through this grating. You always have to figure things out between two bars, and at a distance. I should watch the people going out from the side to be sure. Useless, that's her. I see her. The groups are more and more crowded now. That reassures me. The more there are coming off the train, the more reassured I am. She must be getting closer. A woman in black, with two suitcases. She's coming toward me. No, that's not Hélène. Another: she walks like Hélène. Still, no, Hélène walks more elegantly. Besides, she never wears high heels. Rarely. Well, sometimes. I'm having trouble making out the gaits now. In fact, I no longer know how Hélène walks. Does she carry her shoulders forward? I think not. She doesn't swing in any case; she stays straight. Almost no one is coming now. She is probably having difficulty with her suitcases. Or perhaps she supposes that I am going to meet her on the platform? She did take this train, I hope . . . Yes, surely. You can't mistake the train. Here is a porter, she must be following him. She is too tired to carry her luggage herself. No, that's not her . . . But still. That's impossible.

impossible. Elle ne peut pas s'être trompée à ce point. Ni moi. Une femme au costume noir, aux cheveux courts, et son visage. Elle a dû apparaître dans un groupe et je ne l'ai pas vue, elle a dû passer juste devant moi, ici, à cette grille . . . Ne perdons pas de temps : elle ne peut être loin. Sous ces arcades ? Non. A la grande entrée sûrement. Encore ici une foule. Allons, laissez-moi passer, poussez-vous. Ces Italiens ne fichent rien sur les trottoirs. Pas d'erreur, c'est ici l'entrée. Regardons d'abord à l'intérieur. On ne voit rien soudainement quand on passe du soleil à l'intérieur. C'est encore brumeux. Bon, je distingue les visages. Elle a eu le temps de sortir pendant que ma vue s'adaptait. Elle arrive peut-être à la porte. Hélène, Hélène . . . Ah cette foule m'empêche d'appeler. Cette fois je vais crier plus fort. Hélène ! Elle est ici quelque part, tout près de moi, et je la manque. Elle ne m'entend pas. Ya-t-il de situation plus stupide ? Si cet imbécile de vendeur de billets m'avait laissé passer . . . Bah, c'est aussi difficile sur le quai. Tous les visages affluent tout d'un coup devant moi . . . Il doit y avoir une colonne qui nous cache l'un à l'autre, un mur qui nous sépare. Je me retourne, elle est peut-être derrière moi. Nous brûlons, je le sens. Nous sommes à un instant de nous apercevoir d'un bout de la salle à l'autre ou à travers cette porte ou sur le trottoir d'entrée. Ce n'était pas cet instant, ni le précédent. Ce sera le prochain. Ce taxi barre la vue. Si j'étais moins ébloui quand je passe de la lumière dans cette salle : le temps de reprendre ma vue, elle peut sortir et crier mon nom dehors . . .

Ça y est, j'ai une douleur à l'estomac, un poing. J'aurais dû prendre un café avant de venir ici. Ça creuse la poitrine. Et juste au moment où je comprends qu'il y a deux sorties !!!

Mais pourquoi aurait-elle pris celle-ci si l'autre est plus près.

She can't have made a mistake at this stage. Nor I. A woman dressed in black, with short hair, and her face. She must have shown up in a group and I didn't see her, she must have gone right past me, here, at this grating . . . Let's not waste time: she can't be far away. Under these passageways? No. Surely at the main entrance. Still a crowd here. Let's go, let me through, move along. These Italians just loiter on the sidewalks. No mistake, here's the entrance. Let's start by looking inside. You suddenly see nothing when you go inside out of the sunshine. It's still hazy. Good, I'm making out the faces. She's had time to go out while my vision adjusted itself. Perhaps she's coming to the doorway. Hélène, Hélène . . . Oh, this crowd keeps me from calling out. This time I'm going to shout louder. Hélène! She is here somewhere, very close to me, and I'm missing her. She doesn't hear me. Is there a more stupid situation? If that imbecile of a ticket seller had let me go by . . . Bah, it's just as hard on the platform. All the faces flow past me at once . . . There must be a column that hides us from each other, a wall that separates us. I turn around, perhaps she is behind me. We are burning, I feel it. In a moment we are going to notice each another at opposite ends of the room or through this doorway or on the entrance sidewalk. It wasn't this moment, nor the preceding. It will be the next. That taxi is blocking the view. If I had been less dazzled when I came out of the light into this room: in the time to recover my sight, she could go outside and be shouting my name . . .

That does it, I have a pain in my stomach, a knot. I should have had a coffee before coming here. That sort of thing doubles you up. And just at the moment that I realize there are two exits!!!

But why would she have taken this one if the other is closer.

Cette douleur qui me reprend. On a le sentiment parfois que le corps ne compte plus, et cette douleur précise vient nous rappeler sa présence . . . N'est-ce pas elle qui s'en va ? Hélène, Hélène . . . J'ai pourtant crié assez fort. Elle traverse la piazza Garibaldi. Maudit autobus qui passe devant moi. Hélène ! . . . Où est-elle maintenant ? Je ne la vois plus. Où est-elle ? On ne disparaît pas ainsi. Je l'ai bien vue traverser. Elle marchait vite, avec ses deux valises à la main. Je ne suis pas dans le désert pour avoir des mirages. Je suis en plein milieu de la piazza Garibaldi. Ce n'est pas un rêve ; je ne peux pas me tromper. Evidemment, je l'ai vue de dos . . . Elle était ici exactement, puis soudain, je ne la vois plus. C'est impossible. Elle n'a pas disparu, elle est quelque part. Elle a traversé cette place. Suivons la via Umberto. En avançant vite, je la rejoindrai sûrement . . .

Corso Vittorio, via Roma, piazza del plebiscito, via Cavour . . . Où serait-elle allée que je ne la vois plus. Que doit-elle penser en ce moment ? Elle doit me chercher avec le même désespoir et la même rage. Elle croit peut-être que je suis un ignoble farceur. Cela me flatterait d'avoir le sens de l'humour poussé à cette extrémité de cruauté, mais ce n'est pas le cas. J'en suis même à me demander si ce rendez-vous était clair et net. L'affreux doute que j'ai depuis ce matin et qui se loge dans ce poing dans le ventre où j'encaisse tous les déboires. Comment tout cela peut-il s'accumuler sur moi. Pourquoi ces rendez-vous qui doivent rater sont-ils précisément les nôtres ? Sur les centaines de mille personnes qui se sont revus à la gare aujourd'hui, on aurait bien pu en choisir d'autres pour se manquer. Plus de trois jours que j'attends le train de 10 heures et 40 venant de Rome, et trois semaines que je n'ai pas touché Hélène . . . ,

This pain that takes hold of me again. At times we have the feeling that the body no longer matters, and this exact pain comes to remind us of its presence . . . Isn't that her leaving? Hélène, Hélène . . . Anyway, I shouted loud enough. She is crossing the Piazza Garibaldi. Damned bus passing in front of me. Hélène! . . Where is she now? I no longer see her. Where is she? You don't disappear like that. I definitely saw her cross. She was walking fast, with her two suitcases in her hands. I'm not in the desert seeing mirages. I am right in the middle of the Piazza Garibaldi. This isn't a dream; I can't be mistaken. Obviously, I saw her from the back . . . She was right here, then all of a sudden, I don't see her any more. That's impossible. She hasn't disappeared, she is somewhere. She crossed this square. Let's follow Via Umberto. If I move fast, surely I will catch up with her . . .

Corso Vittorio, Via Roma, Piazza del Plebiscito, Via Cavour . . . Where would she have gotten to that I don't see her any longer. What must she be thinking at this moment? She must be looking for me with the same despair and the same fury. Perhaps she thinks that I'm an unspeakable joker. That would flatter me, to have a sense of humour pushed to that extremity of cruelty, but that's not the case. I'm even asking myself if this rendezvous was plain and clear. My dreadful doubt since this morning, lodging in this knot in my belly where I collect all my frustrations. How can all that pile up on me. Why are our encounters the only ones that have to fail? Out of the hundreds of thousands of people who met again at the station today, others could easily have been selected to miss each other. For more than three days I have been waiting for the 10:40 coming from Rome, and for three weeks I haven't touched Hélène . . . , I didn't

je ne méritais pas cette erreur. Il y en a des milliers d'autres qui auraient pu se tromper plus élégamment que moi. Si quelqu'un veut se moquer de moi ici, je me vengerai ... Le hasard réunit les pires ennemis et nous séparerait. C'est ce maudit hasard qui la fait entrer par une porte pendant que je sors par l'autre. Le hasard fait deux sorties pour une seule gare, des billets de 5000 quand personne n'a de la petite monnaie! Il y a un complot là-dedans. Quelqu'un se paie ma tête ici. Moi pourtant, je ne ris pas, je joue sérieusement. Je ne marche plus avec ce maudit hasard. Ses combines ne m'intéressent plus. Tu peux jouer tout seul à cache-cache. Tu peux t'amuser, si tu veux, à prendre la mauvaise porte au mauvais moment; tu verras, c'est drôle à mourir. On entre par une porte et puis, l'espace d'une fraction de seconde, un coin de colonne, un morceau de mur et le tour est joué: on a raté la seule personne qui existe vraiment. Alors on recommence. C'est aussi distrayant la deuxième fois: on change de colonne et, comme on connaît le jeu, on peut y ajouter du sien: on retarde la confusion, on fait comme si on devait vraiment rencontrer la personne qu'on attend, on hésite, on s'émeut, on craint et puis, à l'instant ultime où on risquerait de la voir vraiment, on sort par la mauvaise porte! Un peu plus et ça y était, on était fini: on se voyait vraiment. Le problème c'est de ne pas se rencontrer, mais en y mettant du sentiment et une certaine élégance dans le désespoir . . . Le hasard est une belle machine pour les amoureux, un joli instrument de supplice. Il suffit de savoir s'en servir et ça fonctionne comme un charme . . . Ah tu peux la garder ta machine, je n'en veux plus, j'ai assez joué, je l'ai montée et démontée vingt fois, j'en connais tout le mécanisme. Je sais exactement comment faire

deserve this mistake. There are thousands of others who could have deceived themselves more elegantly than I. If someone wants to make fun of me here, I will avenge myself . . . Chance reunites the worst enemies and wants to separate us. It's this accursed chance that makes her come in by one door while I go out by the other. Chance has made two exits for a single station, bills for 5000 when no one has small change! There is a conspiracy in this. Someone's pulling my leg here. But me, I'm not laughing, I'm playing for real. I'm not going along with this accursed chance any more. Its schemes no longer interest me. You can play hide and seek by yourself. You can have a good time, if you want, taking the wrong door at the wrong moment; you'll see, you could die laughing. We go in by one door and then, the space of a fraction of a second, a column's alcove, a bit of wall, and this turn is over: we've missed the only person who really exists. So we start again. It's just as entertaining the second time: we change the column and, since we know the game, we can make our own contributions: we delay the confusion, we act as though we were really meeting the person we're expecting, we hesitate, we get excited, we worry, and then at the last moment when we run the risk of actually seeing her, we go out through the wrong door! A little more and that would have been it, we'd have been finished: we'd have really seen each other. The problem is to not meet up, while putting feeling and a certain elegance into the despair . . . Chance is a fine machine for lovers, a pretty instrument of torture. It's enough to know how to use it and it works like a charm . . . Oh you can keep your machine, I don't want any more of this, I've played enough, I've put it together and taken it apart twenty times, I've gotten to know all the workings. I know exactly how to take

pour prendre la mauvaise rue, pour s'adresser à toutes les personnes sauf à la bonne; je connais le mécanisme dans ses moindres détails. Tu peux le garder ton joujou, je te le rends. Moi, je veux rencontrer Hélène pour le vrai. J'en ai assez de frôler les ombres, je veux toucher Hélène, prendre ses mains, ses bras, serrer sa taille, frapper mon corps contre le sien. Ce n'est pas un fantôme que je cherche, mais une femme, grande, forte, noire comme la nuit de l'attente et limpide comme le plaisir de la retrouver. Elle a des yeux lointains et une bouche qui ressemble aux ruisseaux qui descendent des Alpes au printemps, et sa chaleur vaut vingt fois le ciel et l'éternité . . . Non je ne veux plus jouer, je veux Hélène . . . Je vends mon âme à celui qui me la rend!!! M'entends-tu? Je vends mon âme pour la chaleur d'Hélène. A bon marché et sans restriction: mon âme avec mon passé, avec ses nuances et ses calculs, mon âme d'homme faite à la ressemblance de Dieu; ce peu d'éternité qui m'a été accordé, je le vends. C'est à toi que je m'adresse, démon, diable, satan. Je te vends mon âme pour le corps d'Hélène. Tu fais un bon marché. Une âme pleine de vie intérieure et de pensée, 25 ans d'instants les uns après les autres, tout cela pour Hélène, pour la douceur de ses bras, la tendresse de sa peau, la chaleur de son ventre . . . Tout ce qu'il y a d'âme en moi, les moindres soubresauts d'infini, les plus petites parcelles de nostalgie divine, les pensées les plus secrètes, les idées qui me font passer d'une journée à l'autre avec plaisir, les regrets, les remords même sublimes, tout ce qui ressemble, de quelque façon que ce soit à de l'élévation vers Dieu . . . — voilà, prends tout, mais donne-moi ce que j'ai perdu. Rends-moi mon éternité et mon dieu, ces jambes merveilleuses où je m'enroulerai comme du lierre pendant le sommeil, ces cuisses où j'ai trouvé l'infini du repos et la paix absolue, rends-moi

the wrong street, to go up to every person but the right one; I'm acquainted with the mechanism in its finest details. You can keep your plaything, I give it back to you. What I want is to meet Hélène for real. I've had enough of brushing against shadows, I want to touch Hélène, take her hands, her arms, squeeze her waist, bump my body against hers. It's not a phantom that I'm looking for, but a woman, tall, strong, black like the night of expectation and limpid like the pleasure of finding her again. She has distant eyes and a mouth that resembles the streams that come down from the Alps in the spring, and her warmth is worth twenty times heaven and eternity . . . No, I don't want to play any more, I want Hélène . . . I'll sell my soul to whoever restores her to me!!! Do you hear me? I'll sell my soul for the warmth of Hélène. Cheaply and without restriction: my soul with my past, with its nuances and its motivations, my soul of a man made in the image of God; this bit of eternity that has been granted me, I'm selling it. It's you I'm talking to, demon, devil, satan. I sell you my soul for the body of Hélène. You get a good deal. A soul filled with inner life and with thought, twenty-five years of moments, one after the other, all that for Hélène, for the softness of her arms, the delicateness of her skin, the warmth of her belly . . . Everything there is of soul in me, the least starts of infinity, the tiniest particles of divine yearning, the most secret thoughts, the ideas that get me from one day to the next with pleasure, the regrets, even sublime remorse, everything that resembles, in whatever fashion, elevation toward God — there, take it all, but give me what I have lost. Give me back my eternity and my god, those wonderful legs where I will wind myself like ivy during sleep, those thighs where I found infinite repose and absolute peace. Give back to me the

les sables mouvants de son ventre où je m'enfoncerai jusqu'à la mort, c'est sur ce rivage bien-aimé que je veux finir et non dans les portes-tournantes du hasard. C'est sur cet oreiller de sang que je veux appuyer ma tête un moment. Donne-moi ce corps, démon, et mon âme t'appartient pour toujours. Tu en feras ce que tu voudras. Tu la mettras à l'encan, ou tu la revendras, toi aussi, pour le corps d'Hélène! Satan, je t'appelle, réponds-moi vite. Je n'ai pas une minute à perdre. Satan, démon, diable, lucifer, belzébuth . . . la veux-tu mon âme ou tu ne la veux pas? Je te l'offre. Tiens!!! Tu ne me réponds pas? . . . Que veux-tu de plus? Je n'ai plus rien à t'offrir, moi. Mais dépêche-toi, je suis frémissant . . . Ma foi tu me réponds. Ah quel repos, quelle transformation, mes jambes se paralysent, mon sang est plus léger. Je me sens faible; il faut que je m'appuie sur ce mur, sinon je tomberais par terre. As-tu vraiment pris mon âme, toi? Tu es sûr de n'avoir rien oublié? car je ne me sens pas bien du tout. C'est une fatigue étrange, et cette même douleur au côté, ce même poing qui creuse toujours. As-tu bien pris mon âme? . . . Réponds-moi. Si tu as acheté mon âme, rends-moi la monnaie maintenant, je veux ma part, c'est à ton tour de payer. Où apparaî-tra-t-elle? Tu ne me feras pas retourner à la gare n'est-ce pas. Cet endroit me déplaît: ces salles noires, ces doubles sorties, ce système de portes comme s'il ne suffisait pas d'une seule bonne entrée centrale, comme si une porte ne valait pas ce décor de fou avec trois portes, des couloirs, des arcades et partout des écrans pour ceux qui veulent se voir . . . Où la feras-tu apparaître? Devant moi sur le trottoir? . . . Je ne la vois pas pourtant. Je ne vois que ces têtes de Napolitains, ces yeux d'imbéciles qui fixent toujours. Peut-être là devant ce restaurant? . . . Mais je la vois! C'est donc vrai: là, devant

shifting sands of her belly where I will sink until death; it is on this beloved shore that I want to end and not in the revolving doors of chance. It is on this pillow of blood that I want to lay my head for a moment. Give me that body, demon, and my soul belongs to you forever. You can do with it what you want. You can put it up for auction, or you can resell it yourself, for the body of Hélène! Satan, I am calling you, answer me quickly. I don't have a minute to lose. Satan, demon, devil, Lucifer, Beelzebub . . . do you want my soul or don't you? I'm offering it to you. What!!! You're not answering me? What more do you want? I have nothing more to offer you. But hurry up, I've got the shakes . . . Well, you're answering me. Ah what repose, what a transformation, my legs are going numb, my blood runs thin. I feel faint; I have to lean against this wall, otherwise I would fall to the ground. Did you really take my soul? Are you sure you didn't forget something? Because I don't feel at all well. It's a strange tiredness, and this same pain in my side, this same knot that's still aching. Have you in fact taken my soul? Answer me. If you have bought my soul, give me the money now, I want my share, it's your turn to pay. Where is she going to appear? You won't make me go back to the station, will you? That place bothers me: those dark rooms, those double exits, that system of doors as though a single good central entrance wasn't enough, as though one door wasn't worth that insane setting with three doors, corridors, passageways and everywhere screens for those who want to see themselves . . . Where will you make her appear? In front of me on the sidewalk? I don't see her yet. I only see these heads of Neapolitans, these idiotic eyes that always stare. Perhaps there in front of that restaurant? . . . Now I see her! This is for real: there, in front of me,

moi, à l'intérieur du restaurant. Hélène, avec ses cheveux sombres, ses yeux brillants, mais lointains. Elle est noire comme nos chambres d'hôtels à minuit. Je reconnais sa bouche, ses lèvres comme deux lames trempées de sang . . . Elle sort du restaurant. Hélène, Hélène, enfin nous nous retrouvons. Il en a fallu de la chance pour nous rencontrer ici et du malheur pour avoir tant attendu. Hélène c'est moi ! Ne passe pas à côté. Nous avons assez joué à ce jeu depuis le matin, ne me fais plus languir . . . Hélène. Oui, cela était drôle, mais cette fois ne tentons plus le hasard. Ne jouons plus à ceux qui s'égarent, mais à ceux qui se retrouvent: c'est plus drôle. Inutile de te cacher, je t'ai vue. Voilà, touché ! Fini le cache-cache, j'ai gagné . . . Tu me reconnais tout de même ??? Moi, . . . François. Tu veux rire encore. Moi aussi, je veux bien rire . . . Trouvons d'autres motifs . . . Ne te sauve pas, je t'en prie, cela est ridicule. Les bonne farces ne durent jamais longtemps; il faut les écourter au contraire . . . Je t'assure, Hélène, nous devenons ridicules. Arrête. Elle saute dans un tramway. Mais pourquoi fais-tu cela, Hélène ??? *La porta, la porta !* *prego, la porta.* Ouvrez. Je ne veux pas recommencer à courir tout Naples. Ouvrez. *La porta, per favore.* Encore ces maudites confusions de portes: ma vie ne se passera pas aux portes, il faudrait bien entrer parfois ! Hélène. Regarde-moi. Hélène. A l'autre arrêt. Tu vois, je n'ai pas pu monter. Oui, tu descendras à l'autre arrêt. Baisse cette vitre, je veux te parler. Par en haut . . . Baisse la vitre . . . Pourquoi sourit-elle ainsi ? Elle me regarde. C'est toi, Hélène, que j'ai vue cette nuit derrière une vitre. Tu avais ce même air fatigué et ce sourire qui fait mal à la longue. Je le reconnais maintenant ton visage derrière ce mur transparent. Cette vitre donne d'abord l'impression qu'on peut s'entendre et se toucher, puis se moque de nous quand on

inside the restaurant. Hélène, with her dark hair, her bright but distant eyes. She is black like our hotel rooms at midnight. I recognize her mouth, her lips like two blades drenched in blood . . . She's leaving the restaurant. Hélène, Hélène, at last we've found each other. It was lucky that we met here and unfortunate that we had to wait so long. Hélène, it's me! Don't pass me by. Enough! We've been playing at this game since morning, don't keep me dangling any longer . . . Hélène. Yes, that was amusing, but this time let's not go on tempting chance. Let's not pretend any longer to lose our way, but to find each other again: that is more amusing. No use to hide, I've seen you. There, bingo! Hide and seek is over, I've won . . . Surely you recognize me??? Me, François. You still want to laugh. Me too, I really want to laugh . . . Let's find some other reasons . . . Don't run off, please, that's ridiculous. Good jokes never last long; they need to be cut short instead . . . I assure you, Hélène, we are becoming ridiculous. Stop. She is jumping on a streetcar. So why are you doing that, Hélène??? *La porta, la porta! Prego, la porta.* Open up. I don't want to start running all over Naples again. Open up. *La porta, per favore.* Again these blasted confusions with doors: my life can't be spent at doorways, you just have to get through sometimes! Hélène. Look at me. Hélène. At the next stop. You see, I wasn't able to get on. Yes, you'll get off at the next stop. Lower this glass, I want to talk to you. From the top . . . Lower the glass . . . Why is she smiling like that? She's looking at me. It's you, Hélène, that I saw last night behind a pane of glass. You had this same tired look and this smile that hurts in the long run. I recognize it now, your face behind this transparent wall. At first this glass gives the impression that we can hear and touch each other, then it makes fun of us when we

s'y frappe. Je vais la briser cette vitre, je la ferai sauter en miettes et alors tu sauras qui je suis. Alors tu entendras le vrai son de ma voix et tu verras la vraie couleur de mes yeux. Jusqu'à maintenant il y avait toujours cette glace, ce miroir à double tranchant où je me déchirais. En miettes, en milles morceaux égaux, en poussière; il ne restera plus rien entre nous. Tu me verras pour le vrai désormais. Evidemment, avec cette fenêtre fermée par le haut et le bruit du tramway . . . , mais tu te rappelleras tout d'un coup tous nos gestes. Oui, d'un seul coup, quand j'aurai fait sauter la vitre, tous ces instants te reviendront. En un sens, c'est presque normal que tu aies oublié un peu . . . la fatigue du voyage, le dépaysement, l'arrivée à Naples et le bruit du tramway. J'aurais dû te laisser une photo de moi, car après trois semaines et en plein jour c'est déjà difficile de se reconnaître . . . Si je peux rejoindre ce tramway maintenant. Je ne cours pas après les tramways tous les jours; ça me donne des poings partout. Heureusement qu'il avance comme un corbillard. Je vais le rattraper au prochain arrêt. J'arrive, j'arrive . . . Hélène, c'est moi!!! Tu ne me reconnais pas? Mon visage ne te rappelle rien, non? Tu ne revois pas sur mes bras nos nuits d'amour??? Les voilà nos nuits d'amour, je vais les faire jaillir en mille étoiles. Me reconnais-tu maintenant. Il y a encore des vitres. Il faut que je brise tout cela. Il faut que je me déchire les mains pour écarter ce rideau. J'emplirai le ciel de ces miettes, j'en couvrirai le visage de tous ceux que je déteste, j'en ferai de la poudre pour farder Dieu, je lui en mettrai sur les joues et sur les tempes et, au moment où il ne me regardera pas, je lui en mettrai plein la bouche pour le faire étouffer. Ça lui fera des raies de sang dans le palais et il sera longtemps sans parler, il bafouillera et crachera le sang comme un pulmonaire . . .

strike against it. I'm going to break this glass, I'll make it fly into bits and then you'll know who I am. Then you'll hear the real sound of my voice and you'll see the real colour of my eyes. Up till now there has always been this cold plate glass, this two-edged mirror where I was lacerating myself. Into bits, into thousands of equal pieces, into dust; nothing will remain between us any longer. You will see me for real from now on. Obviously, with this window latched at the top and the noise of the streetcar . . . but all of a sudden you'll recall all of our interactions. Yes, all of a sudden, when I have sent the glass flying, all those moments will come back to you. In a sense, it's almost normal that you would have forgotten a little . . . travel fatigue, dislocation, getting to Naples and the noise of the streetcar. I should have left you a photo of myself, since after three weeks and in broad daylight it's already hard to recognize each other . . . If I can overtake this streetcar now. I don't run after streetcars every day; I have knots everywhere. Fortunately it's moving along like a hearse. I'll catch up with it at the next stop. I'm coming, I'm coming . . . Hélène, it's me!!! Don't you recognize me? Doesn't my face remind you of anything? Don't you see again on my arms our nights of love??? There they are, our nights of love, I'm going to make them burst forth in a thousand stars. Do you recognize me now? There are still panes of glass. I have to smash all of that. I have to lacerate my hands to push aside this curtain. I'll fill heaven with these bits, I'll cover the face of all those I hate, I'll make them into a cosmetic for God, I'll put some on his cheeks and temples, and in the moment when he isn't watching me, I'll cram his mouth full to choke him. That will streak his palate with blood and he won't be able to speak for a long time, he'll splutter and spit blood like a consumptive . . .

SHIFTING SANDS / 65

Tant qu'il y aura des vitres intactes, je ne serai pas heureux, car elles m'empêchent de voir. Je les briserai toutes avec mon poing, comme ça . . . Et maintenant, Hélène, regarde moi. Il n'y a plus d'écran entre toi et moi. Reconnais-tu celui qui s'est couché avec toi dans un grand lit immobile. Mes cheveux, mes yeux, mon visage, mon corps nu et déchiré par le désir. Alors Hélène, tu ne me souris plus ? Mais qu'est-ce que tu as maintenant ? Tu n'es plus la même. Ton visage a changé. Ma foi, tu deviens laide. Ton sourire est croche, tes lèvres galeuses, tes yeux ressemblent à des boules de sang noir, le pus coule sur tes seins . . . Pourquoi me regardes-tu ainsi ? Tu ne voulais pas que je brise cette vitre ? Où sont ton sourire de tout-à-l'heure, tes cheveux ardents, ta bouche merveilleuse . . . Ce n'est donc pas toi. Pourtant, je le sais. J'ai encore le goût de tes baisers dans ma bouche, je me souviens de l'odeur de ta peau. Tout cela ne peut mentir. C'est impossible. Mais tu es laide, affreusement laide. Tes yeux surtout sont laids. Ta bouche est sale et je ne peux croire que j'y ai posé mes lèvres si souvent. Souris encore, de grâce. Souris, je te l'ordonne, que je sois enfin persuadé de ta laideur. Ah, je te déteste. Tu es laide. Je vais te couvrir de vitre toi aussi: je vais planter du verre dans tes prunelles, je vais te farcir le ventre de petits morceaux coupants, je te caresserai avec ces nouvelles griffes et tu saigneras. Je t'enfermerai sous une ampoule de verre et chaque baiser que je te donnerai la fera éclater en mille miettes sur ton visage; chaque fois que je soupirerai vers toi, tu recevras des éclats de verre. Quand je te caresserai, tu te sentiras couper à l'intérieur. J'entrerai en toi hérissé de crochets, je déchiquèterai ton ventre, je mettrai ton âme en lambeaux et je la vendrai comme j'ai vendu la mienne . . . pour un reflet dans une vitre. Le Maudit m'a remboursé avec du faux, tu paieras pour lui.

As long as there are panes of glass intact, I will not be happy, because they keep me from seeing. I'll smash them all with my fist, like this . . . And now, Hélène, look at me. There is no more screen between you and me. Do you recognize the one who slept with you in a large motionless bed. My hair, my eyes, my face, my body naked and torn by desire. So, Hélène, won't you smile at me any more? What's with you now? You aren't the same any more. Your face has changed. My goodness, you're getting ugly. Your smile is crooked, your lips scabby, your eyes look like balls of black blood, pus is running over your breasts . . . Why are you looking at me like that? Didn't you want me to break this glass? Where is your smile from a little while ago, your fiery hair, your wonderful mouth . . . Then this isn't you. But I know it is. I still have the taste of your kisses in my mouth, I remember the smell of your skin. All of that cannot lie. That's impossible. But you are ugly, hideously ugly. Your eyes especially are ugly. Your mouth is filthy and I can't believe that I put my lips there so often. Smile again, for pity's sake. Smile, I command you, so I'll be convinced once and for all of your ugliness. Oh, I hate you. You are ugly. I'm going to cover you with glass too: I'm going to stick splinters of glass in the pupils of your eyes, I'm going to stuff your belly with sharp little pieces, I'll caress you with these new talons and you'll bleed. I'll shut you up in a glass bulb and each kiss I give you will make it burst into a thousand bits on your face; each time I sigh at you, you will get bursts of glass. When I caress you, you'll feel yourself being cut inside. I'll enter you bristling with hooks, I'll shred your belly, I'll tear your soul in tatters and I'll sell it the way I sold mine . . . for a reflection in a pane of glass. The Accursed One has settled accounts with a cheat, you'll pay for him.

Car il faut que je me venge. Je me suis condamné à tout détester à jamais et tu seras mon univers.

Hubert Aquin

Palerme, Siracuse, Agrigente, Taormina, Naples, Rome, mai 1953.

Because I have to get even. I have condemned myself to hate everything eternally and you will be my universe.

Hubert Aquin

Palermo, Syracuse, Agrigentum, Taormina, Naples, Rome
May 1953

NOTE ON THE TITLE

FOR HUBERT AQUIN, the title words of his 1953 novella develop to become a node of associations, a leitmotif, a locus of obsession. This early story incorporates a single occurrence of the phrase at a point of climax. Lost in internal dialogue, the narrator François conceives a Faustian bargain, to trade his soul for the body of Hélène, so he can pursue the act of generation to the point of dying: "Give back to me the shifting sands of her belly where I will sink until death" (*Rends-moi les sables mouvants de son ventre où je m'enfoncerai jusqu'à la mort*.)

Considered in isolation, the collocation *sables mouvants* seems quite ordinary, a usual equivalent to "quicksand" or possibly the slightly unusual plural, "quicksands." In the Aquin cosmos, however, the term may entail a self-contradictory dryness, and for this reason

the English translation of the title has been rendered as "Shifting Sands." The substances that dominate *Shifting Sands* (plaster, marble, stone, and glass) yield dust and sand and lacerating shards. At the first use of the word *vitre* (glass), the source manuscript indicates abandonment of the word *fenêtre* (window). What seems likely here is a play between *vitre* (glass) and *ventre* (belly). The word *vitre* also emphasizes glass as a substance.

The phrase *sables mouvants* recurs in each of Aquin's following four novels over the span of a decade of writing. His next use embeds the image in an explicit desert scene. The narrator of *L'invention de la mort* (1959/1991) meditates on love as the captive of time, eternal only in impassioned memory,

> in the way that pyramids are eternal in the middle of the desert. And still, pyramids founder slowly in their parched earth, they glide from year to year with all their weight, because all sand is shifting. (13 [translated from French ed.])

The paragraph ends with the narrator's thoughts retracing his route against the current to arrive at the woman's face that started everything. (A paragraph a few pages earlier wanders from rumination on Oedipus and the Sphinx to an anticipation of interviewing visiting Egyptian dignitaries — the narrator is a journalist.)

In *Next Episode* (1965), the narrator starts from a dream of "totalitarian art in constant genesis." The predominant theme here is revolution and the history of Quebec. The web of associations extends to the act of writing, to suicide, and to sexual intercourse:

> From that contradiction no doubt come the wild fluctuations in what I write, a frenzied alternation of drownings and resurfacings. . . . Our history will be launched in the blood of a revolution

that is breaking me, that I've served poorly: on that day, with slashed veins, we'll make our debut in the world. On that day, a bloody intrigue will build on our quicksand an eternal pyramid that will let us measure the size of our dead trees. . . . The revolution will come the way love came to us one June 24 when, naked and glorious, we annihilated each other on a bed of shadow while a conquered people was learning how to march in step. (64–65)

Both of the passages in *Blackout* (1968) start from ordinary quicksand in an expected topography:

Just like me to lose myself as well and wander hopelessly amid the faults of the littoral, along a sunken coast that calls to me and strangles. . . . Yes, my homeland is no other than these shifting sands which imbed Lagos in its jewel-case of bluffs. Born of the sand, I try interminably to take root there, but I sink down and find my prison in the filigree of the littoral and the deltaic calligrams of the shoreline. (79)

I am sucked down, no less, into those quicksands which — according to the visionary descriptions of this "author" — lie coiled about the Island of Lagos like an evil spell. . . . I find myself strangling without a scream. It all ends in a kind of disorder that is too strong for me, and I am overpowered by a malarial inspiration that transforms me into a writer! A writer I die, and burrow into a black, lagoon-shaped grave, while. . . . (96)

In this context the salient associations are the act of writing, the sense of being lost, constraint, and death.

The two passages in *The Antiphonary* (1969) occur in close succession:

No bounds, indeed; my sadness knows no bounds, it is measureless, endless, bottomless and irreversible. The more I sink into it the less possible it is to extricate myself. My sadness is a veritable

quicksand, viscous and soft . . . [ellipsis sic] in my own image (114).
I, of course, am beautiful neither in my flesh, nor in secret, nor in
my body nor through chastity. All these cistercian connotations of
woman's beauty are denied me. I could die of it. I am in constant
agony, I feel myself caught in the moving and viscous sand that
for me takes the place of solid ground. (115)

Theological overtones colour expressions of melancholy, suffering,
and death. Regrets attenuate the ecstasy of physical love to an abstract
catalogue of flesh, body, chastity, and woman's beauty.

Aquin's associations with *sables mouvants* appear to progress from
energy to lassitude, from primary engagement with a female other
to overwhelming sadness, from conjuration of revolution to anomic
solipsism, from prolific writing to the inertia of unfinished work. His
body of self-expression may indeed realize the trajectory announced
by François to Hélène at the end of *Shifting Sands*:

I have to get even. I have condemned myself to hate everything
eternally and you will be my universe.

WORKS CITED

L'invention de la mort. Éd. critique. [Saint-Laurent, Québec]: Bibliothèque
    québécoise, 2001.
Prochain épisode. Éd critique. [Saint-Laurent, Québec]: BQ, 1995.
Next Episode. (Sheila Fischman, tr.) Toronto: McClelland & Stewart, 2001.
Trou de mémoire. Éd. critique. [Saint-Laurent, Québec]: BQ, 1993.
Blackout. (Alan Brown, tr.) Toronto: Anansi, c. 1974.
L'antiphonaire. Éd. critique. [Saint-Laurent, Québec]: BQ, 1993.
The Antiphonary. (Alan Brown, tr.) Toronto: Anansi, c. 1974.

THE MALEFICENT VISION
AND *SHIFTING SANDS*:

A Critical Essay by Joseph Jones

∞

IN *SHIFTING SANDS*, the narrator François awaits the arrival of his beloved, Hélène. His surroundings in Naples mingle with his memories, fancies, and anticipations. Toward the end of the story, François sees frightful visions of Hélène's face in a glass.

In the closing episode of *Shifting Sands*, the fundamental element is the unsettling reflection of a face. Variations of such a scene can be found in many authors. The reflection often appears in a window, whose glass offers the doubleness of seeing oneself while seeing the face of an *other* behind the surface. The disturbing face is often distinguished by a distortion of the mouth, frequently described as a smile or a grin. Sometimes noted as features are whiteness or pallor, and certain expressions in the eyes. An experience of seeing the

reflected face tends to accompany a crisis, both an exterior event and an interior dislocation. The mental state of the viewer may involve dreaming and a blurring of ego boundary. Witnessing a primal scene or participating in a sexual encounter sometimes constitutes the immediate circumstances. Seeing such a face portends evil and death, and the face may be perceived as that of the devil. Consequent actions may include smashing the reflecting surface, falling ill, and suffering or committing murder or suicide. As a literary form, the scene seems more extensive than an image, and more diffuse than a topos. In some cases the scene, or aspects of the scene, multiply within the narrative. As the scene recurs in the works of different authors, its nature comes to seem more a matter of repetition and of individual psychology than one of appropriation and development within literary tradition. Nevertheless, literary embodiments of the scene permit comparison at the level of form.

⌕ TWO PREVIOUS STUDIES OF THE THEME

Two previous studies of this theme, unrelated to one another, deserve particular mention. The longer and more recent of the two, C.F. Keppler's *The Literature of the Second Self*, offers a review of preceding studies and attempts to typologize instances of the double in literature. Much of the book consists of the paraphrasing and summarizing of literary works that have been grouped into various categories. A primary concern with literary representation leads Keppler to focus on matters of form, rather than on the psychological speculation common to studies of the double. Keppler's key perception is that the very notion of "second self" entails a necessary and unresolvable paradox: self that perceives self as other in some measure ceases to be self, even as it recognizes something other as being iden-

tical with self. In the most relevant chapter, "The Vision of Horror," an evil second self menaces the self without being active as pursuer or tempter. This chapter does not remark on the disconcerting mouth as a feature of the vision, even though *The Picture of Dorian Gray* (to be considered later) serves as one of its examples. Another chapter, "The Second Self as Beloved," also proves suggestive for *Shifting Sands*. What becomes the maleficent vision is also what has been remembered and awaited as the beloved. The crossover found in Aquin's novella demonstrates the permeable nature of the boundaries that separate Keppler's categories.

W.H. McCulloch's earlier and shorter treatment of the theme starts from an event in the life of Percy Shelley. His essay opens with three accounts of an incident that occurred at Tanyrallt. The first narrative of that incident, apparently drawn from the cited account of Margaret L. Croft, says that Shelley "fancied that he saw a man's face on the drawing-room window; he took his pistol and shot the glass to shivers, and then bounced out on the grass, and there he saw leaning against a tree the ghost, or, as he said, the devil." McCulloch finds that Shelley's state of mind illustrates "a conclusion which I had already formed from experience and reading: that adoring narcissism, double-going and suicide are three stages in, or aspects of, a unified process." In an account of his own experience of seeing a menacing reflection, McCulloch describes these facial features: "a smooth or haggard darkness, an evil, feline expression . . . a satyr-like smile . . . a fiercer smile . . . with the lower jaw forced open against the tension of the lips and the eyes widened." McCulloch closes with mention of a series of dreams that "began abruptly at a time when, having passed through the development of adoring narcissism with almost all the features I have described, I was subject to

a powerful impulse to suicide, the threat of which was perceived by others before I recognized it myself." McCulloch's account then turns from autobiographical phenomenology to literary instances drawn from Stevenson, Maupassant, Poe, and Shelley (these are added to an earlier passing mention of Goethe). A concluding section analyzes at length a reproduced copy of a sketch made by Shelley at the time of his experience. Shelley's drawing shows a grinning diabolical face adjacent to a reflecting square shape.

∞ AQUIN'S "TRAGÉDIE DE L'AMOUR"

Direct literary context for the writing of *Shifting Sands* can be found in Aquin's journals, notably in the 1952 entries for September 30 and October 1, 14, 18, 20, 22 (133–138). Here Aquin contemplates the aesthetic requirements that would govern "la tragédie de l'amour" in novel form (132, 137). Of interest are two passing literary references that precede and follow this set of entries. The first appears in the entry for August 26, where Aquin says that he is obsessed by two models, and goes on to express his desire to represent (in a different literary project) "l'intensité de la mort d'Anna Karénine" (129). A listing of plays recently seen suggests that this reference to Anna Karenina derives from a theatrical version seen in May 1952 (98). In the novel, Anna Karenina commits suicide by throwing herself under a train. Shortly before, when she contemplates separation from Vronsky, suicide occurs to her as she sits before a mirror. Advent of the thought brings "a fixed smile of compassion for herself" (VII.24:745). A little later Anna feels threatened by Vronsky's smile, and then goes to a pier-glass to check her hair. There she experiences a moment of dissociation:

"Who is that?" she thought, looking in the mirror at the inflamed face with strangely shining eyes fearfully looking at her. "Ah, it's me," she realized, and looking herself all over, she suddenly felt his kisses on her and, shuddering, moved her shoulders. Then she raised her hand to her lips and kissed it. (vii.27:755)

Aquin's use of a train station setting may owe something to Tolstoy. The second passing literary reference appears in a journal entry for December 19, where Aquin quotes a line from Shelley's "Stanzas Written in Dejection, near Naples." Shelley is an author with an experiential connection to the scene of interest, and the title of the poem — Naples — names the setting of Aquin's work.

∞ OSCAR WILDE'S *THE PICTURE OF DORIAN GRAY*

Comparative comment on *Shifting Sands* will follow a brief exposition of two other novellas that present a maleficent vision. The first of the two, Oscar Wilde's *The Picture of Dorian Gray*, likewise involves a Faustian bargain.

It seems likely that Wilde's novella forms a part of the reading out of which Aquin wrote *Shifting Sands*. In two later fictions, Aquin's narrators make explicit reference to Dorian Gray. Draft textual material associated with *Trou de mémoire* (307) mentions Dorian Gray in a context of viewing writing about a dead child through a "vitrine" (glass case). Closer in time to *Shifting Sands*, and more resonant, is a scene in *L'invention de la mort* (17–18). The narrator recalls the "vertige" brought on by completely undressing his beloved: "son corps, à mes yeux, ne lui ressemblait pas. . . . J'avais soulevé le voile qui recouvrait le portrait de Dorian Gray" (her body, to my eyes, did not resemble her. . . . I had lifted the veil that covered the picture of

Dorian Gray). In his beloved's naked body, the narrator perceives signs of the pervasive death emphasized by the novel's title.

Wilde's novella tells the story of attractive and wealthy young Dorian Gray, whose life becomes entwined with his remarkable portrait. Something mysterious causes the portrait to express Gray's physical aging and moral deterioration while Gray himself remains unchanged. In painting the picture, the artist has sensed an interaction between his work and its subject. The first event in Gray's self-indulgent slide to destruction is his courtship of lower-class actress Sybil Vane. A proposal of marriage causes her sudden loss of the dramatic ability that had drawn Gray to her. Gray's consequent rejection drives her to suicide. The ambivalence of this self-destructive attraction and rejection bears a similarity to the relationship between François and Hélène in *Shifting Sands*.

At the point of Sybil Vane's suicide, Gray discovers the first sign of degradation in the face of the painting and locks it away in a disused upstairs room. Shortly afterward, the painter asks Gray to sit for him again and to allow exhibition of the portrait. Gray's refusal ends their relationship and, incidentally, destroys the painter's talent. The passage of years is conveyed by an account of the influence of a strange book, interlaced with mentions of Gray's unsavoury activities. The painter visits to confront Gray about the life he has been leading. This leads to a viewing of the portrait, a situation that impels Gray to murder the painter. Disposal of the body requires blackmail, and the blackmailed acquaintance subsequently commits suicide. On a visit to an opium den, Gray narrowly avoids dying at the hand of the brother of Sybil Vane. Thereafter, Gray lives in fear of the avenger, until his pursuer happens to die in an accident. Gray remains haunted by the possibility that his murder of the painter

will come to light. Sparing an innocent village girl, Gray attempts self-reform, but he can only see his effort as hypocrisy. With the same knife that killed the painter, Gray stabs the portrait that records the state of his soul. His own body with a loathsome face is then discovered beside an unsullied portrait.

A troubling face pervades this novella in the form of the picture that reflects Dorian Gray's degrading soul. The first perceptible change is "a touch of cruelty in the mouth" following his rejection of Sybil Vane. Gray checks his own face in a nearby mirror: "No line like that warped his red lips" (7:119). He comes to recognize, "What the worm was to the corpse, his sins would be to the painted image on the canvas" (10:149). The painter, on his fatal final visit to Gray, perceives in the portrait "the face of a satyr" and "the eyes of a devil" (13:190). Gray is moved to the murder by something "whispered into his ear by those grinning lips" (13:192). Waiting for assistance in disposal of the painter's body, Gray finds that his fears manifest themselves as "the imagination, made grotesque by terror, twisted and distorted as a living thing by pain, danced like some foul puppet on a stand, and grinned through moving masks" (14:201). At the close of the story, Gray reacts to a reflection of his own face: "He loathed his own beauty, and, flinging the mirror on the floor, crushed it into silver splinters beneath his heel" (20:260). Just before the attack on the portrait that translates into suicide, and after his attempt at a good action, Gray sees in the portrait "no change, save that in the eyes there was a look of cunning, and in the mouth the curved wrinkle of the hypocrite" (20:261).

In the suicides of actress Sybil Vane and accomplice Alan Campbell, the narrative offers faint repetitions of the central action. Gray's murder of painter Basil Hallward amounts to a kind of suicide as

well. At the level of passing image, the faces of avenger James Vane and abandoned village girl Hetty Merton appear misty and white in windows. These multiplications are scarcely noticed when set alongside Gray's fate and the portrait itself. In *Shifting Sands*, François recalls various episodes with Hélène: an evening, the next morning, another evening. Any sense of sequence or progression in these events succumbs to a confused multiplicity reinforced by François's intermittent wandering in the streets of Naples.

Beyond manifestations of disturbing faces, and reinforcing narrative duplications, two other features of this novella deserve elaboration: the action of Gray that seems to trigger his bond with the portrait, and the strange connection between Hallward and Gray. Both make use of language that has religious overtones.

On first looking at the completed portrait, Dorian Gray regrets his own mortality:

> If it were I who was to be always young, and the picture that was to grow old! For that — for that — I would give everything! Yes, there is nothing in the whole world I would not give! I would give my soul for that! (2:49)

Later, when Dorian Gray has the first inkling that his Faustian proposal has taken effect, he recalls his "mad wish" (7:119). Much later, in his final encounter with the painter, Gray says, "I made a wish, perhaps you would call it a prayer" (13:190). At the end he regrets the "monstrous moment of pride and passion [in which] he had prayed that the portrait should bear the burden of his days" (20:260).

The peculiar interrelationship of painter and subject emerges in two passages. At the outset, the painter Basil Hallward recalls his first meeting with Dorian Gray:

When our eyes met, I felt that I was growing pale. A curious sensation of terror came over me. I knew that I had come face to face with someone whose mere personality was so fascinating that, if I allowed it to do so, it would absorb my whole nature, my whole soul, my very art itself. (1:28)

In the scene that leads to the rupture in the relationship between Hallward and Gray, the painter offers a "strange confession":

I was dominated, soul, brain, and power by you. You became to me the visible incarnation of that unseen ideal whose memory haunts us artists like an exquisite dream. I worshipped you.

Hallward goes on to describe his attitude as "idolatry." Ultimately the artist is said to have been blasted by seeing "perfection face to face" (9:144–146). In some sense Hallward's perception of Gray recapitulates Gray's perception of his own portrait.

∞ J. MEADE FALKNER'S *THE LOST STRADIVARIUS*

Like *Shifting Sands*, J. Meade Falkner's *The Lost Stradivarius* has a Neapolitan setting. Although there is no evidence that Aquin was acquainted with this novella, the story's setting and scene and detail offer further perspective on the themes of *Shifting Sands*. (The resolution of Falkner's tale provides my succinct terminology — maleficent vision — for the unsettling experience whose scene recurs in often unrelated fictions.)

Artistic motifs stand prominent in all three novellas. Visual art provides the central portrait device of *The Picture of Dorian Gray*. A musical instrument coupled with a mesmerizing melody serve a similar transcendental function in *The Lost Stradivarius*, reinforced by a frightful painting. In the more compressed circumstances of

Shifting Sands, art within the narrative itself becomes far more tangential — the writing that Stendhal would have done in the place of François, a museum masterpiece like the Mona Lisa subjected to scorn. In the background of these stories, muses act as harsh mistresses.

The narrative of *The Lost Stradivarius* is presented as an account written by Sophia Maltravers. As explained in a prefatory letter, she provides the story to her nephew on his coming of age, as her deceased brother John has requested. Further detail of past untoward events comes in an appended and much shorter account by college friend William Gaskell.

After several years at Oxford, a friendship develops between John Maltravers and William Gaskell, rooted in their common love of music. Gaskell returns from a trip to Italy with some seventeenth-century Italian scores. The two fall into the habit of playing a particular piece, which is accompanied by the peculiar creaking of a wicker chair. One evening as they play the piece, John sees "some slight obscuration, some penumbra, mist, or subtle vapor which . . . seemed to struggle to take human form" (2:12). It is a week before they can play again, and at that time Gaskell describes a scene of Italian revelry that the music brings to his mind. Sophia visits Oxford in the company of Constance Temple, who captures her brother's heart. After their departure, John plays the piece of music by himself late at night and perceives an actual human figure. The perception causes him to experience a "profound self-abasement or mental annihilation" and to feel "combined reverence and revulsion." Seen in detail, the figure's complexion was "very pale or bloodless" and the "finely cut mouth, with compressed lips, wore something of a sneering smile" (3:22). The friends separate for vacation. Back at home,

John tells everything to his sister Sophia. Just before his return to college, they play the piece of music together, and Sophia notices on the cover of the score a coat of arms described in Gaskell's scene. Back at college, John has a bookshelf moved in his room and discovers a cabinet containing a Stradivarius. Concealing the discovery from his friend and his sister, John confirms the quality of his discovery with a London dealer.

Over Christmas vacation John and Sophia visit the Templetons. About to propose to Constance, John suddenly sees the figure that has appeared to him while playing the music, and he faints and falls ill. Sophia discovers that a lightning flash has illuminated the portrait of a wicked ancestor named Adrian Temple, who disappeared in Naples almost a century ago. John's description and Sophia's experience reiterate the key features: "his face waxen pale, with a sneering mouth" (8:58), "his mouth was sharply cut, with a slight sneer on the lips, and his complexion of that extreme pallor" (8:61). John and Sophia remain at the Templetons as John recovers. Sophia notices in the portrait a scroll bearing notes from the piece of music. John finishes at Oxford and plans are made for his marriage to Constance. John's relationship with Gaskell has virtually come to an end with his discovery of the violin. A six-week honeymoon stretches to three months as the couple lingers in Naples, where John has taken ill.

At his return in December, John appears "strangely pale" (10:82). Since leaving Oxford John has shut himself away and obsessively played the piece of music on the violin. John abandons his customary religious observances. In March, John returns alone to Naples with his valet, but his short stay is brought to an end by Constance's pregnancy. Toward the end of July, John makes a surprising attempt to play his music with Constance, but breaks it off in dissatisfaction

and leaves her very upset. Late that same night Sophia and Constance find John playing before the portrait of Adrian Temple. The next morning John departs for Naples. Shortly after that, Constance dies. About a year later John writes to Sophia that he is ill, and he asks her to come to Naples. Once there, Sophia wanders into a series of caves, experiences a "feeling of undefined horror" (13:111), and learns that they are called the cells of Isis. The local "medley of things sacred and profane" (13:113) disturbs her. John takes Sophia to visit a place that he has managed to identify with the scene envisioned by Gaskell. At the foot of a winding subterranean staircase lie the remains of Adrian Temple. John and Sophia return to England. John shows some improvement and makes connection with his son and his friend Gaskell. John sleepwalks, plays the fatal tune on the Stradivarius, and the violin breaks with a "horrible scream." Shortly afterward John dies.

The note from Gaskell that follows the account of Sophia adds detail and speculation to her narrative of events. Having come to visit at John's request, Gaskell learns that John has not told Sophia of finding Adrian Temple's diaries together with the violin. Gaskell studies the diaries and observes the absence of three leaves. Eventually Gaskell determines that the missing leaves must contain Temple's account of a "deadly experiment" (162). More than a page goes into considering the evidence provided by the "deadly pallor" of John, the "white and waxen face of his spectral visitant," and Adrian Temple's report that his companion "went out from my presence with a face white as snow" (155). While dozing, Gaskell has "a succession of fantastic visions" (157), in one seeing John reciting incomprehensible words while "another man with a sneering white face" (158) plays the violin. John attempts to convey the contents of the

missing three leaves to Gaskell, then attempts to tell him their location, but dies before anything can be communicated. Gaskell arrives at this conclusion: "I can imagine that the mind may in a state of extreme tension conjure up to itself some forms of moral evil so hideous as metaphysically to sear it" (162). Gaskell goes on to advert to "the legend of the visio malefica . . . a converse to the beatific vision" (163).

∞ THE MALEFICENT VISION IN *SHIFTING SANDS*

Salient differences separate the maleficent vision presented in *Shifting Sands* from those of the two novellas just outlined. Time is compressed. The three-day agony of François's wait for the arrival of Hélène compares with the years of downward trajectory experienced by Dorian Gray and John Maltravers. The narrator of *Shifting Sands* inhabits a world in which other characters have little substance, and that world is refracted through the perceptions of a first-person narrator who is also the central character. *The Picture of Dorian Gray* is recounted by an omniscient third person, while *The Lost Stradivarius* distances its central mystery through the limited perspectives of two witnesses to the events. The role of explicit religious elements is far more direct in *Shifting Sands*, which features a deliberate Faustian bargain and an assault on God himself. (The presence of a character named Hélène recalls earlier versions of the Faust tale.) More in the background are Dorian Gray's almost inadvertent "mad wish" coupled with passing mentions of sins, prayer, incarnation, worship, and idolatry. Even further in the background, John Maltravers discontinues usual religious observance as he becomes obsessed with his vague pagan pursuits.

Perhaps the most striking difference between the two novellas

and *Shifting Sands* lies in the content and extent of their maleficent visions. That of *The Lost Stradivarius* remains largely undefined, with intimations conveyed through the portrait of Adrian Temple and his emanation. By his actions, John Maltravers becomes something of a double for what is seen of Adrian Temple. Most of the horror is left offstage. The maleficent vision of *The Picture of Dorian Gray* resides primarily in Gray's picture, whose subjective link to its original breaks down the distinction between self and image. In these two stories, the beloved ones — Sybil Vane and Constance Temple — occupy a secondary position in the narrative and lack direct connection with the horrors seen by their suitors. Even so, each woman dies as a result of her association with the man who loves her. In *Shifting Sands*, François remains focused throughout on Hélène. No other character plays a significant role. Quite a few references are made to Hélène's mouth and lips, and to a pane of glass that renders her inaccessible. At the end of the story, Hélène's absence becomes entangled with a maleficent vision of what has earlier been the beloved. François attacks the glass that separates him from Hélène's smiling face, and then uses the fragments of glass as weapons. (This attack ties in with the already mentioned attack on God.) An intimation of this denouement has come in a bored challenge to the Mona Lisa (a painting with an enigmatic smile) and to God while sitting at a café. Afterward, in a premonitory dream, François finds himself beating his own face bloody against a glass that separates him from Hélène. When François sees Hélène with "lips like two blades drenched in blood," the story turns toward its apocalyptic conclusion. After the narrator refers to a "two-edged mirror where I was lacerating myself," an injuring of the subject shifts to an injuring of what has the appearance of the formerly beloved object. Equipped

with talons and hooks, the attacker comes to resemble the devil, as the frightful beloved herself takes on demonic aspect. Distinctions collapse in solipsism.

A minor aspect of *Shifting Sands* becomes clearer through comparison with Nathaniel Hawthorne's "Monsieur du Miroir." Although this whimsical sketch steers wide of an openly maleficent vision, its narrator remarks about M. du Miroir: "I would as willingly exchange a nod with the Old Nick" (398). On two occasions there are telling smiles. At one point the narrator complains that M. du Miroir has "never . . . whispered so much as a syllable" and must be possessed by a "dumb devil" (396). To the previously explored visual manifestations of isolation can thus be added an auditory dimension. In his recollections of Hélène and his encounters with visions of her, François suffers particular distress at her silence and at their inabilities to speak and hear.

∽ SEXUAL ENCOUNTER AS CONTEXT
   FOR THE MALEFICENT VISION

The three novellas considered above share a reticence that reflects the socio-historical conditions attending those literary works (late Victorian England and mid-twentieth-century Quebec). Although *Shifting Sands* has a predominant concern with one specific sexual relationship, Aquin's narrator does not go very far verbally in this early work. Almost as soon as François undresses Hélène, his narrative shifts to religious metaphor and fades into ellipsis:

> J'aspirais ses seins brûlants: c'était mon pain et mon vin, ma nourriture la plus indispensable. . . . (I inhaled her burning breasts: this was my bread and my wine, my most indispensable food. . . .)

When François pursues the memory further, a more explicit continuation climaxes in religious metaphor:

> Je sondais les parois de cette chappelle ardente, j'emplissais ces lieux sacrés de ma force et de mon plaisir. C'était une voûte de cathédrale qu'emplissait mon chant et l'écho me revenait en même temps. (I sounded the walls of that candle-lit funeral chapel, I filled those sacred places with my strength and my pleasure. It was a cathedral vault that my chant filled, and the echo came back to me at the same time.)

Recollection of a later encounter takes a similar turn:

> Je l'embrassai. J'avais le sentiment de retrouver un paradis que ma folie m'aurait fait perdre. . . . . L'amour est comme le célèbre voleur de l'évangile. (I kissed her. I had the feeling of regaining a paradise that my madness would have caused me to lose. . . . . Love is like the celebrated thief of the gospel.)

Even though François's descriptions tend toward religious metaphor, sexual encounter is central to the circumstances of maleficent vision in Aquin's novella.

∽ ROBERT MUSIL'S *THE MAN WITHOUT QUALITIES*

A comparative look at a major twentieth-century novel illuminates this aspect of the theme. Linkage of a sexual encounter with elements of the maleficent vision pervades Robert Musil's *The Man Without Qualities*. (A subplot of the novel revolves around a notorious case of murder by a character named Moosbrugger — the brutal murder being his reaction to what he perceives as a "soft, accursed second self" (74).) The multiple sexual relationships of protagonist Ulrich, the titular man without qualities (or self-unmade man), occasion the emergence of various characteristics of the maleficent vision.

In an especially concentrated scene, Ulrich stops short of consummating a sexual encounter initiated by the young and inexperienced Gerda Fischel (Ch. 119, "A Countermine and a Seduction"). Throughout the event, both participants experience themselves as deeply double-minded. At the outset Gerda views herself in a mirror. When Ulrich follows Gerda to bed, he finds himself frightened rather than attracted:

> He found, not, of course, any feeling of love, but a half-crazy anticipation of something like a massacre, a sex murder or, if there is such a thing, a lustful suicide, inspired by demons of the void who lurk behind all of life's images. (678–679)

Gerda's unwilled hysterical screams come "from lips that grimaced and twisted and were wet as if with deadly lust" (679).

> This revolt of her body against herself was frightful. She perceived it with utmost clarity as a kind of theater, but she was also the audience sitting alone and desolate in the dark auditorium and could do nothing to prevent her fate from being acted out before her, in a screaming frenzy. (679)

A second female character becomes a prominent nexus for features associated with the maleficent vision. Ulrich's married friend Clarisse is almost as central to the novel as Ulrich himself. At the level of narrative, she displays a fixation with the criminal Moosbrugger and eventually seeks to visit him in prison. She possesses "a velvety-black birthmark . . . in the hollow of her groin" that she calls "the Devil's Eye" (318, 475). Clarisse makes two widely separated sexual attempts on Ulrich (a strong instance of narrative doubling).

The first incident is interrupted by the sudden return of Clarisse's husband. "Clarisse's usual smile, that funny little grimace" (382) gave

way to "a smile that curled on her lips like an ash left behind in the wake of the burned-out flare from her eyes" (383).

> "It's occurred to me more than once that you're the Devil himself!" These words had slipped out of Clarisse's mouth like a lizard. . . . Ulrich caught a flicker in her eyes; she wanted him. Her upturned face was suffused with something — nothing at all lovely, something ugly but touching. Something like a violent outbreak of sweat blurring the features. But it was disembodied, purely imaginary. He felt infected by it against his will and overcome by a slight absentmindedness. (387)

The second incident occurs at a structural crux of the narrative, the final chapter of the novel's second part (ch. 123, "The Turning Point"). Clarisse tells Ulrich that she wants a child from him, and goes on about how Ulrich is the devil. The previous incident leads Ulrich to anticipate a repulsive face that he is surprised not to find:

> In a moment her face will be drenched with that look, like the last time, Ulrich thought apprehensively. But nothing of the kind happened; her face remained beautiful. Instead of her usual tight smile there was an open one, which showed a little of her teeth between the rosy flesh of her lips, as though about to bite." (718)

Clarisse then goes into action. Ulrich

> had never yet seen Clarisse in such a state of sensual excitement. . . . Clarisse suddenly made a physical assault on him. . . . Her words were no more than a raving murmur at his ear . . . a rippling stream of sound in which he could only catch a word here and there, such as "Moosbrugger" or "Devil's Eye." In self-defense he had grabbed his little assailant. . . . "I'll kill you if you don't give in," she said loud and clear. . . . She struggled on in mounting excitement. (720–721)

These three scenes from *The Man Without Qualities* incorporate many elements of the maleficent vision — looking into a mirror, strange smiles, explicit diabolical references, states of dissociation, intimations of murder and suicide, and violent physical assault. In other circumstances Ulrich undergoes several extraordinary experiences that integrally evoke or involve mirror or window (299, 389, 686). Ulrich's sister Agathe — with whom he develops an incestuous relationship — engages in the novel's most extensive episode of straightforward mirror-gazing:

> It had begun by accident with her face, when her gaze had landed on it and not come back out of the mirror. . . . She was held captive, without vanity, by this landscape of her self, which confronted her behind the shimmer of glass. (926)

Later in that episode, Agathe makes "an ecstatic face" (927) while looking into the mirror. Her mirror-gazing experiences provoke her to examine a capsule of poison and then to pursue extensive and convoluted thoughts of death.

In conclusion, the world of *Shifting Sands* — a world both claustrophobic and spatially disorienting — has a reality at the level of impersonal substances, where plaster, marble, stone, and glass yield a universe of dust and sand and lacerating shards. Left behind are flower, vegetation, forest, garden, plant, fountain, gesture — and most of all, the body. The narrative features an extensive catalogue of names for parts of the body. In the single phrase from which the story's title is drawn, "les sables mouvants de son ventre" (the shifting sands of her belly), "les sables mouvants" might be taken as quicksand or quicksands. However, arguing against that understanding is the dryness of the materials that are fundamental to the imagined

world of the story, especially when those materials are coupled with the glassy punning on the belly: *vitre* (glass) and *ventre* (belly). (In *L'invention de la mort* (13) a more explicit desert atmosphere encompasses an occurrence of the phrase "sables mouvants.")

From contemporary journal entries, it appears that Aquin set out to write a "pure tragédie de l'amour." Viewed in the light of the two novellas selected for comparison, *Shifting Sands* reduces narrative distance, concentrates time, and eliminates extraneous characters. Self struggles directly with other self, while "God" moves from background convention to integral factor in the equation. Boundaries grow fuzzy. Love becomes a passion that insists on continuing to look, even to the paradoxical point of its own destruction.

WORKS CITED

Aquin, Hubert. *L'antiphonaire*. Éd. critique (т. 3, v. 5). [Saint-Laurent, Québec]: BQ, 1993.

Aquin, Hubert. *L'invention de la mort*. Éd. critique (т. 3, v. 2). [Saint-Laurent, Québec]: Bibliothèque québécoise, 2001.

Aquin, Hubert. *Journal* 1948–1971. Éd. critique (т. 2). [Montréal]: BQ, 1992.

Aquin, Hubert. *Trou de mémoire*. Éd. critique (т. 3, v. 4). [Saint-Laurent, Québec]: BQ, 1993.

Croft, Margaret L. "A strange adventure of Shelley's and its belated explanation," *Century Magazine* 70:6 (Oct. 1905): 905–9.

Falkner, John Meade. *The Lost Stradivarius*. Oxford: Oxford University Press, 1991.

Hawthorne, Nathaniel. "Monsieur du Miroir," pp. 395–405 in *Tales and Sketches*. New York: Library of America, c. 1982.

Keppler, C.F. *The Literature of the Second Self*. Tucson: University of Arizona Press, c. 1972.

McCulloch, W.H. "The incident at Tanyrallt on the night of 26 February, 1813," *Explorations* 3 (Aug. 1954): 105–19.

Musil, Robert. *The Man without Qualities* (translated by Sophie Wilkins). New York: A.A. Knopf, 1995. 2 v.

Tolstoy, Leo. *Anna Karenina* (translated by Richard Pevear and Larissa Volokhonsky). London: Penguin, 2001, c. 2000.

Wilde, Oscar. *The Picture of Dorian Gray*. Harmondsworth: Penguin Books, 1985.

NOTES ON THE EDITION
AND TRANSLATION

THE FRENCH TEXT is transcribed from a single typescript of thir-ty-three leaves held at the Université du Québec à Montréal, Service des archives et de gestion des documents. That manuscript is desig-nated in the Fonds Hubert Aquin as 44P-660:02/2 and bears the handwritten title *Les sables mouvants* (along with the designation "nouvelle" and the year "1953"). Textual variation and emendation (apart from single-letter strikeovers and multiplication of spaces) are recorded in a separate listing keyed to the text. Several substantial variants have interest for interpretation. Editing is conservative, with minimal correction and regularization. Aquin's Italian is reproduced without alteration. Chronological discrepancy and allusion occasion a few notes on content.

The translation is conservative, starting from faithfulness to the original, yet respecting the requirements of readable English literary prose. Alterations to syntax and punctuation of the source text are minimal.

Thanks are owed to literary executors Andrée Yanacopoulo and Emmanuel Aquin for making the text available and for agreeing to its translation and publication. Stephanie Jones facilitated two stays in Montreal. Thoughtful suggestions from Hélène Meloche Redding improved the rendering of the French into English. Stylistic review by Jeanette Jones improved both the English translation and the accompanying essays. Further suggestions from Ronald Hatch and Anne Scott made the texts even better.

∞ ABOUT THE TRANSLATOR

Living in Aquin's Montreal, Joseph Jones witnessed the impacts of the October Crisis at first hand. Coming to Quebec from the Carolinas to the south, he found a striking resemblance between "Je me souviens" and "Forget? Hell!" Despite being a generation younger than Aquin, he relishes as familiar territory the mid-century timescape of *Shifting Sands*.

Librarian emeritus at the University of British Columbia, Jones marked the close of that stage on his life's way with the publication of *Reference Sources for Canadian Literary Studies*. He has turned from keeping the books of others to making his own.

ANNOTATIONS

Chronological discrepancies: 13:09 "she'll be here at 1:40" | 33:11 "she arrives at 11:30" | 49:21 "It's eleven-ten. Just thirty minutes and the train will be there." | 55:27 "the 10:40 coming from Rome"

25:18   "the magic isle . . . Voices called me . . ." — Allusion to the sirens of the *Odyssey*?

25:26   "candle-lit funeral chapel" [chapelle ardente] — Chapel where a deceased person is viewed, often lighted by candles.

43:05   "the celebrated thief of the gospel" — Luke 23:39–43

59:11   "I'll sell my soul" — This pact resembles that of Faust, who also seeks an Hélène, Helen of Troy.

ANNOTATIONS

Discordances chronologiques: 12:09 "elle sera ici à 1.40" | 32:10 "elle arrive à 11.30 heures" | 48:21 "Il est 11 heures et dix. Trente minutes seulement et le train sera là." | 54:27 "le train de 10 heures et 40 venant de Rome"

24:18   "L'île magique . . . Des voix m'appelaient . . ." — Allusion aux sirènes de l'*Odyssée*?

24:26   "chapelle ardente" — Salle où l'on veille un mort, souvent éclairée de cierges.

42:06   "le célèbre voleur de l'évangile" — Luc, 23, 39–43

58:11   "je vends mon âme" — Ce pacte ressemble à celui de Faust, qui cherche aussi une Hélène, Hélène de Troie.

NOTES SUR LE TEXTE /
NOTES ON THE TEXT

∽

[ ]   Biffé dans le tapuscrit / Crossed out in the typescript

< >   Addition ou correction supralinéaire /
       Addition or correction above the line

~~???~~ Non déchiffré / Not deciphered

10:02   Ça | Ca

10:06   de me broyer | deme broyer

12:12   je n'ai le goût | je n'ai [plus] le goût

12:23   Ces murs bruns laids. | Ces murs bruns laid.

12:25   leurs grandes pattes | leurs grandes pattes [partout]

12:26   ce sont les vraies araignées | [il y a des] <ce sont les> vraies araignées

14:03   doit être | doitêtre

14:05   trou de serrure | trou[v] de serrure

14:07   fois qu'Hélène | fois [que] qu'Hélène

14:10   quelqu'un ne passerait | quelqu'un passerait

14:11   Elle l'a regardée | Elle l'a regardé

14:24	plaisait. Et avec	plaisait Et avec
14:26	avec elle. C'est moi	avec elle, C'est moi
16:01	la pente. Devant	la pente. [Même] Devant
16:02	devenais	[d]devenais
16:04	le même, peut-être désinvolte	le même, Peut-être désinvolte
16:18	sauf, seul avec Hélène	sauf, Seul avec Hélène
16:19	évident quoique,	évident[,] quoique,
16:28	que j'avais remarquée	que j'avais remarqué
18:03	effleurée	effleuré
18:06	ce visage avec	ce visage[a] avec
18:09	un traître mot.	un[e] traître mot.
18:10	ces baisers faciles:	ces baisers [aisés] <faciles:>
18:16	mouillées	mouillés
18:21	La devinant consentante,	La [sentant] <devinant> consentante,
18:22	dégrafai	dégraffai
18:24	Elle se laissait	Elle se[l] laissait
18:27	poitrine palpitante	poitrine [pa???] palpitante
20:12	le métro . . .	le métro. .
20:22	passion.	passion[s].
20:28	impossible.	impossible, [et prenait la scè]
22:07	jour d'araignées.	jour [à]d'araignées.
22:12	aisément	aiséement
22:16	ma tête. Je dors	ma tête. [Je suis pris dans] Je dors
22:20	je deviendrai nid	je deviendrai [un] nid
24:03	les yeux	ses yeux
24:05	Je m'appuyais à ce balcon étrange	Je m'appuyais [à cette courbe puissante où pouvait s'accrocher la rade des hommes] à ce balcon étrange
24:18	la magie de l'île	la magie de [cette] <l'>île
24:23	pourtant me bouleversait	pourtant <me> bouleversai[en]t
24:26	chapelle ardente	chappelle ardente
26:06	que mes souvenirs	que me souvenirs
26:11	tordue	torudue
26:15	J'essaie de garder	J'essaie [de me rappeler du poid] de garder
26:19	peut-être? . . .	peut-être? . .
28:04	Pas un seul aveu	Pa un seul aveu
28:05	je ne me trompe pas.	je ne me trompe[e] pas.
28:10	de trouver	detrouver
28:21	au moins, quelques mots	au moins., quelques mots

28:24   à me dire, une chose | à me dire., une chose

30:07   improbables. | inprobables.

30:08   ses cuisses, | [c]ses cuisses,

32:01   À toutes | A toutes

32:05   Italien | italien

32:05   lâche | lache

32:28   comme un | commeun

34:22   j'ignore encore ce qui | j'ignore encore ce [qu'y] qui

36:03   sable. | sable. [Alors, il poussera bien quelque fleur dans ces ruines . . .]

36:12   regarder nulle part | regarder[n] nulle part

38:09   comme si la lumière | comme [s'i] si la lumière

38:14   fortement, | fortement [dans mes bras],

38:20   être | etre

40:04   mots qui avaient précédé. | mots qui avaient [été prononcés] précédé.

40:07   privation | pprivation

40:12   l'embrassai. | l'embrssai.

40:14   la fraîcheur | la fraîcher

40:23   jamais retrouvé | jamais retrouver

42:02   ceux qui requièrent | ceux qui [ont besoin] requièrent

42:04   le rituel, je les plains. | le rituel, [ej] je les plains.

42:10   Cet instant | [C'es] Cet instant

42:21   la fraîcheur de ta bouche | la fraîcheur de [ton visage] ta bouche

44:04   en avant même . . . | en avant même. . . .

44:05   qu'il faisait froid, que nous | qu'il faisait froid [et], que nous

44:07   drôle | drole

44:11   le métro ensemble | le métro[p] ensemble

44:25   connaître . . . | connaître. . . .

44:26   dix heures et demie! | dix heures et demi!

46:01   une vitre | une [fen] vitre

46:06   La vitre était | La vitre[é] était

46:07   transparente. Hélène | transparente. [Elle n'enten] Hélène

46:10   Je me déchirais | Jeme déchirais

46:11   comme ce matin-là | comme[ce ma] ce matin-là

46:23   doit avoir passé Formia | doit avoir passer Formia

48:03   il direttissimo | il [rap] direttissimo

48:13   25 lires | 25 lire

48:14   conducteur? — "Je | conducteur? Je

48:14   Je vous prie | Je vous[en] prie

48:14	faire" — Le	faire. Le
50:02	Questo . . . , da	Questo, . . . da
50:05	Non . . . , non . . . , non . . . , pas elle, non . . .	Non . . . . , non . . . . . ,
	non . . . . . , pas elle, non	
50:07	Une femme! . . . non.	Une femme! . . . . non.
50:11	visage d'ailleurs.	visaged'ailleurs.
50:22	avant? Il	avant? il
50:26	se tromper	se trouper
52:01	s'être trompée	sêtre trompée
52:05	ces arcades? Non.	ces arcades? non.
52:18	retourne, elle est peut-être	retourne elle est peutêtre
52:21	le précédent.	leprécédent.
52:25	Ça	Ca
52:26	Ça	Ca
52:27	sorties!!!	sorties!!!!
54:01	On a le sentiment	On le sentiment
54:05	maintenant? Je	maintenant? je
54:10	Evidemment, je	Evidemment, [elle etait de] je
54:15	via Cavour . . . Où serait-elle allée	via Cavour. . . . Où serait-elle allé
54:17	la même rage.	la meme rage.
54:18	peut-être	peut-etre
54:19	flatterait	flatterai
54:19	extrémité de cruauté	extrémité de [ma] cruauté
54:20	même	meme
56:03	vengerai . . . Le hasard	vengerai. . . . Le hasard
56:04	hasard qui la fait	hasard qui [l'a fait] la fait
56:08	je ne ris pas,	je ne rie pas,
56:26	la garder ta machine	la garder [t a] ta machine
58:10	l'éternité . . . Non	l'éternité. . . . Non
58:12	rend!!!	rend!!!!
58:12	M'entends tu? Je	M'entends tu? je
58:16	m'adresse, démon	m'adresse démon
58:25	Dieu . . . — voilà,	Dieu. . . . — voila,
60:02	bien-aimé	bienaimé
60:02	finir et non dans	finir et [dans] <non> dans
60:09	ou tu ne la veux pas?	ou tu la veux pas?
60:09	Tiens!!!	Tiens!!!!!
60:10	pas? . . . Que	pas? . . Que
60:11	frémissant . . . Ma	frémissant. . . . Ma
60:12	se paralysent, mon sang	se paralysent[m], mon sang

60:15	oublié? car | oublié[?] car
60:20	Tu ne me feras pas | Tu[j] ne me feras pas
60:21	ce système | ce[s] système
60:26	têtes de Napolitains, | têtes de[s] Napolitains,
62:01	restaurant. Hélène | restaurant. "Hélène
62:13	rire . . . Trouvons | rire . . . trouvons
62:24	que j'ai vue cette nuit | que j'ai vu cette nuit
64:01	miettes | mietttes
64:08	rappelleras | rappeleras
64:09	j'aurai | j'aurai[s]
64:12	photo de moi, car | photo de moi, [Tu me verras distinctement bientôt] car
64:15	ça me donne | éa me donne
64:27	Ça | Ca
66:02	m'empêchent de voir | m'empêchent de[e] voir
66:08	galeuses | galleuses
66:09	boules | boulles
66:11	Où sont ton sourire | Où [est] <sont> ton sourire
66:14	de ta peau. | de ta[p] peau.
66:14	Tout cela ne peut mentir. | Tout cela n[m]e peut mentir.
66:24	Quand je te caresserai | Quand te je caresserai

HUBERT AQUIN
(1929–1977)

∞

NÉ ET MORT À Montréal, Hubert Aquin a fait toutefois de nombreux séjours à l'étranger, spécialement à Paris et en Suisse. Il est aujourd'hui considéré par le Québec et par le Canada comme l'un de leurs plus grands écrivains. Il s'est intéressé à la radio et à la télévision, ainsi qu'au cinéma: il a, pendant plusieurs années, travaillé à l'Office national du film du Canada et signé entre autres un film sur le sport avec des commentaires de Roland Barthes, le grand critique et sémiologue français.

Mais ce sont surtout ses romans qui l'ont fait connaître, et plus particulièrement *Prochain épisode*. Cet ouvrage a été accueilli à sa parution (1965) par une critique enthousiaste: «Nous le tenons enfin, notre grand écrivain», écrit Jean Ethier-Blais, cependant que Gilles Marcotte intitulait son article: «Prochain Épisode, une bombe!». Noter que cet ouvrage se vend à raison d'environ 1500 copies par an — ce qui pour le Québec

HUBERT AQUIN
(1929–1977)

∞

THOUGH HE WAS born and died in Montreal, Hubert Aquin spent much time abroad, especially in Paris and Switzerland. Today he is considered by Quebec and by Canada as one of their greatest authors. He took an interest in radio and television, as well as in film; for a number of years he worked for the National Film Board of Canada. His films included one on sport with commentary by Roland Barthes, the great French critic and semiologist.

But above all else he is known for his novels, and more particularly *Next Episode*. This work was greeted in 1965 by an enthusiastic critic. "We have him at last, our great author," wrote Jean Ethier-Blais — while Gilles Marcotte entitled his article: "*Next Episode*, a Bomb!" It is to be noted that this work has sold regularly at the rate of about 1500 copies a year since its appearance — which for Quebec

et ses sept millions d'habitants est un chiffre important — et ce, très régulièrement depuis sa parution en 1965.

Quant aux autres romans, les reconnaissances officielles n'ont pas manqué: Prix du Gouverneur Général pour *Trou de mémoire*, son deuxième roman (prix qu'il a refusé), Prix de La Presse (le plus grand quotidien français d'Amérique) pour *l'Antiphonaire* (son troisième roman), Prix de la Ville de Montréal pour *Neige Noire* (son quatrième et dernier roman). Enfin, il a reçu en 1972 le Prix David, décerné à un écrivain par la province de Québec pour l'ensemble de son œuvre. Par ailleurs, l'Université du Québec à Montréal a donné son nom à l'un de ses pavillons, et Jacques Godbout a tourné sur certains aspects de sa vie un documentaire d'une heure intitulé *Deux Épisodes dans la vie d'Hubert Aquin*, diffusé à plusieurs reprises à la télévision d'État et visionné dans des salles publiques de cinéma. Enfin, un buste d'Aquin (exécuté par le sculpteur Arto) était, jusqu'à il y a peu, logé dans la grande salle de la Bibliothèque nationale du Québec.

Depuis sa mort (honorée le 15 mars 1977 à l'Assemblée Nationale du Québec par une minute de silence), l'œuvre d'Aquin a fait et continue de faire l'objet de nombreux articles de revue et de thèses universitaires, non seulement ici mais en France, en Italie, en Allemagne etc., tous pays dans lesquels elle est enseignée. Une Édition critique, parrainée conjointement par l'Université de Montréal et l'Université du Québec à Montréal, et dirigée par Bernard Beugnot, est à la disposition des chercheurs (11 volumes).

Notons, entre autres, une entrée dans le dictionnaire français Robert des noms propres, et une page entière consacrée à l'écrivain par le *Dictionnaire des littératures de langue française* (3 volumes), édité en France par Bordas.

Pour plus de détails et de précisions, voir Guylaine Massoutre, *Itinéraires d'Hubert Aquin*, Montréal, BQ, 1992.

Andrée Yanacopoulo

and its seven million inhabitants is a significant figure.

As for the other novels, official recognition has not been lacking: a Governor General's Award for *Blackout*, his second novel (an award that he refused); Prix de La Presse (the largest French daily in America) for *The Antiphonary*, his third novel; Prix de la Ville de Montréal for *Hamlet's Twin*, his fourth and last novel. Finally, in 1972 he received the Prix David, bestowed on authors by the Province of Quebec for their entire body of work. In addition, the Université du Québec à Montréal named one of its buildings in his honour. Jacques Godbout shot a one-hour documentary on certain aspects of his life: *Two Episodes in the Life of Hubert Aquin*, broadcast several times on public television and previewed in movie theatres. Lastly, a bust of Aquin (executed by the sculptor Arto) was until recently housed in the great hall of the Bibliothèque nationale du Québec.

Since his death (acknowledged March 15, 1977, in the Assemblée Nationale du Québec by a minute of silence), Aquin's oeuvre has been and continues to be the object of numerous journal articles and academic dissertations, not only here but in France, Italy, Germany and elsewhere — all countries where his work is taught. A critical edition of 11 volumes (sponsored jointly by the Université de Montréal and the Université du Québec à Montréal, and overseen by Bernard Beugnot) is available to researchers.

Among other entries can be noted one in the French encyclopedia Robert of proper names, and an entire page devoted to the author in the three-volume *Dictionnaire des littératures de langue française*, published in France by Bordas.

For additional details and particulars, see Guylaine Massoutre, *Itinéraires d'Hubert Aquin* (Montreal: BQ, 1992).

Andrée Yanacopoulo

Recycled
Supporting responsible use
of forest resources
FSC   www.fsc.org Cert no. SGS-COC-003153
© 1996 Forest Stewardship Council

Marquis Book Printing Inc.

Québec, Canada
2009

This book has been printed on 100% post consumer
waste paper, certified Eco-logo and processed chlorine free.